DOORWAYS

Dr. Yousef El-Kaddar

Doorways

Cover photo: Filip Kominik on Unsplash
Book design: Gray Dog Press

ISBN: 978-1-7374941-0-2

Printed in the United States of America

Dedication

This labor of love is dedicated to
my beloved wife, Karen Benner El-Kaddar,
the Editor of "Doorways"

Contents

Prelude

Long time ago when I was a young man my father said to me, "Yousef, you like to write stories."

I said, "Yes, I do."

"Someday when you are ready you might write stories about the emotional power of life," he said. "Sometimes life makes choices for us. Life is an acquisition of memories and in the end that's all there is."

"Write and let the chips fall where they may!"

"No, don't write and let the chips fall where they may," he said. "Write stories with strands of fiction that no one can say where fact ends and fantasy begins."

"I will think deeply about it, Father."

"Pick a memory from here, pick a memory from there, add them together, you get a good picture."

"I will remember that, too."

"Physical objects can vanish without trace, but not memories. Stroll down a memory lane, and only then you will understand what happened and why. You make a memory, you earn a memory—everything old is new again," my father said.

Doorway One

The Derwishes

A Myth

It has been said that during the summer of 1850 there was a man named Khandaburro Derwish, who was eighty years old, existing in the desert; and spent all his life alone in the desert, wandering through it in search of water. No one ever knew from where he came from or found his past key to unlock his roots either. He never married nor had any friends, except the sky—his lifelong companion. After years of roaming through the endless miles of the desert sands, while hunting over the dismal desert for its treasured water, he finally settled in a region named Sharshara—an area consists of, an ancient land with a few sandstones and palm trees, then. By the forces of the sky, he was given again a lifeline, granted the gift to rule over the land of Sharshara. He was seven feet tall, slim built, pale brown skin tone, and had a noticeable hunchback.

His face was like an ancient prickly pear, and his eyes and head gleamed like sand dunes kissed by the sun. He was destitute of necessaries of life; he had only the clothes on his back, tent, and a companion of a camel named Vamoose, as his means of transport to travel across the desert. He was able within a short period of time to establish a permanent foothold in his new location.

One morning while he was sitting underneath a palm tree, leaning up against its trunk, a voice emerged from the sandstones, and echoed in his mind, "Water is the life for all nature." He began to ponder how to unearth the water in the new land—his heart was detached in many ways from the earthly life and attached to the heavenly life.

The next day, he rose early before the first ray of the sun rose up and headed straight to the spot of the sound sandstones—it was ten minutes in distance from his tent. He began to dig under the sandstones with both of his brawny bare hands searching for nature's gift of water, hoping against hope that he would discover water. As he kept digging, the freshly dug soil became muddy and muddier and the water began to filter upward. He returned to his tent to rest, hoping for the best. A few hours had past, he returned back to the promising hole with his leather bucket; and when he reached the promising hole, he discovered the underground water had risen to the surface. He bowed his head over the pool of water as he was immensely grateful. He took a full bucket of murky water from the hole, lifted it on his broad shoulders, and began to return back to his tent.

While he was walking with the slimy water bucket, a voice not from the sandstones this time, but from the blue above, the sky said, "Khandaburro, stop here . . . place the bucket on the ground and sprinkle water on this spot, after you make a wish in your heart, in your heart." He stopped dead in his tracks and wished he had varieties of vegetables and fruits; then he splattered the cherished water over the soil, and returned back to his tent, hoping against hope once more that he would find his wishes to become a reality.

On the second day he went back to the place where he splashed the precious water over the ground; he paused and couldn't believe his two eyes—he saw a bountiful harvest of fresh vegetables and fruits were springing up at his bare-feet. What surprised him even more was when he saw a small pond, with its water racing over the soil in the place where the pit was first dug. He shook his head in wonderment, stared up at the sky with beseeching eyes and rising arms, "O Heaven, I am speechless and trembling with delight for your artistry and your gifts. I am so grateful for your mercy and your kindness. I am very thankful for your water and your food. You are the most graciously generous, far too generous with your offerings. You are the protector of the sky and the provider of all creation. You are the most kind-hearted and the most generous of all. You are the most forgiving for our sins, and have mercy on us." He invoked. Then, he began swirling around himself like a child's spinning top and clapping his right-hand fingers against his left back hand while he was invoking. He twirled around himself quickly enough invoking the entire invocation with rejoicing tears until he became unconscious. Within seconds, he lost his balance and collapsed onto the ground.

Six months later, a trade caravan, with many camels carrying men and goods, on their winter trade trip, found him lying on the ground beside a dead camel. When the convoy approached him, they thought he was lying on the ground resting in peace—his eyes were open and transfixed upward to the sky, his face was radiating strength, and his body was fragrant. But when they approached him they discovered him dead as the dust of the desert. The sun-bleached skeletal remains of the dead camel were partially covered in sand without any unpleasant scent. The wise-elder man of the convoy, Krozac, said that the camel died after the death of his owner. Someone said if your words are to be true, why didn't his dead body decompose? Krozac said whether you want to admit it or not, I am sure that the man died before his camel; I don't know the man and I don't know his name either, but I am quite sure that he was a reformer; and I am quite certain that he was the one who brought water and greenery to this region, as there was neither water nor greenery in the past years. They buried the unknown deceased man the same day, next to his tent, and then they placed a large stone as a marker over his grave. Respectively, they took care of the remains of the camel as they covered it with the endless desert sand.

They were twenty caravan riders; they spent a few days and nights in the same location, where they ate ample amounts of dates from the plentiful date palm trees; and consumed vast quantities of tomatoes, onions, cucumbers, and watermelons from the vast desert garden of their departed host. After such a strenuous journey, traveling in the sweltering heat of the desert, the riders drank small-scale amounts of water as the dead man's fresh-water pond quenched their once endless thirsts better than any other water in the arid desert. They slept that night under the watchful eyes of the stars except for Krozac, who slumbered in the tent of the late unnamed man. The nighttime brought an essence of tranquillity, and during the night the wise elder, Krozac, had an obscure vision—he saw, in his dream, a glowing mass of light in the shape of a tall person with a hunchback spinning around himself, while he was shaking a tambourine.

The very next morning, Krozac rose early to greet the sunrise and quickly returned to the anonymous man's gravesite. His eyes became unspeakably wide in wonderment when he came face to face with the grave—a carving on the large stone, which read, "Khandaburro Derwish" was real and evident as the first morning rays of daylight. He then realized that the deceased man wasn't just an ordinary human being, he was a miraculous man. He believed that Khandaburro Derwish was a life-long reformer, who was descended from the sky to leave behind his irreplaceable footprints on the desert sands.

It was beyond any question, when they placed the stone upon his grave the previous day it was untouched of any carving. They all stood in front of his gravesite, looking puzzled and asking themselves; how could this be and who carved his name on the stone? The only person who had an answer to their questions was the wise caravan elder, Krozac. He explained to them that this is clearly a miracle and clear sign from the heavens, that he was an honorable man; and I have no question that he was the one who unearthed the water out of the depths of the earth; and no doubt that he was the one who planted the fruits (cucumbers, pumpkins, tomatoes, and watermelons) and the vegetables (carrots, corn, garlic, onions, and potatoes); and he who cared for the date palm trees and maintained its growth and prosperity in this desert region. They knew from his answer that he had the knowledge of the unseen world, he knew the unknown. Plus, they knew he was such a paragon of virtue. His reply was a sufficient and a healing conclusion, which made them ready to continue their journey through the desert.

When they strapped their bundles of goods (as much as 200 pounds) upon their camels, something out of the ordinary occurred. Four camels of the twenty camel herd including Krozac's camel refused to stand and remained crouching on the sand. There Krozac looked around at his fellow riders, scrutinized over them, and said, "This is a heavenly sign; the four camels who abstain from standing, including mine, must stay on this land with their owners, I, Shug, Rosco, and Bolanos; the rest you will have to continue your journey without us," continued Krozac, "the land gussied up with its water and vegetation. We are the chosen ones to remain here, planting and growing plants for food; and raising animals for their meat and milk. We are now the chosen caretakers of this blessed land."

They stayed tuned and waited for three days watching over the four camels which were crouched on the ground, refused to lurch upward. On each day, the same four camels did so, resisted to rise when the rest of the herd were on their soft padded feet, ready to move onward. Finally, the convoy left the area leaving behind Krozac, Shug, Rosco, and Bolanos.

Krozac was seventy-five years old, tall and thin with short white hair, sun-shinning face with deep blue set eyes; Shug was seventy-three years old, short and stout with short salt-pepper hair, brown spots on sun-exposed face with hazel eyes; Rosco was seventy-two years old, short and stocky with grayish hair, dark face with brown eyes; and Bolanos was seventy years old, tall and slender, with wavy black hair, very tanned face with dark brown eyes. All of them wore similar clothing for the desert climate; which consist of baggy white pants; a length-knee baggy white shirt; white skull cap; and rubber slippers. They were decent men and had a paragon of living by a code of purity and chastity.

As the hands of the time went on, the four men got more accustomed with their new lifestyle, to the point that they realized that nothing in life is impossible, apart from death. They established a home base station for caravans, offering free water to travellers and their animals. At first, they traded their services for chickens. Then they began to trade the sun-dried fruits such as dates, tomatoes for sheep and goats; the fleece of the sheep, and the hides of the sheep, goats, gazelle, and foxes for camels. The area was transformed during the course of time from a mere halting-place for caravans to an oasis, a green locale with a bountiful supply of water in the desert. Those four men were regarded as the revered pioneers in establishing an oasis in the desert.

Months had passed and months went by without any disruption in their daily routine or lifestyle. They labored from dawn till dusk, and as dusk fell, they always retired to their tents. The four co-workers were normal in that respect until one evening. That same evening, five women accompanied by a man, up in his years, with a well-groomed white beard came out of nowhere and appeared at the flap opening of Krozac's tent. The elderly man was barefooted and was wearing a long white tunic and a white head-cloth; the women were wearing white trousers, white long-sleeved tunic blouses reaching their ankles, they veiled their faces with white veils, and none of them wore any shoes. The elderly man introduced himself as Zoltar, and the women as Zeena, Gwyneth, Sabrina, Dahlia, and Angelique with no apparent last names. Krozac greeted them at the entrance flap of his tent and gave them a wordy welcome as a gesture of goodwill. The elderly woman, Zeena, was Zoltar's wife; and the four young women were their daughters. The host was an admirable example of being hospitable, heaping an ample plate of dates and serving warm goat's milk for them. Although, they were conservatively polite, in partaking, they ate some dates and drank some of the goat's milk.

When Krozac asked to see their camels, the elderly man's eyes glanced up and said that they have no need for camels, and they descended from the sky. Krozac shivered as he heard the strange response from the unusual strange guest.

The elderly man noticed Krozac's fear upon his face, and said instantly, in his serene voice, "Fear my dear sir, weakens the kidneys, anxiety weakens the stomach, and tension weakens the heart plus one's mind; scatter at once all the human nature negative emotions, they will gang up upon you, one by one. We are envoys from heaven; don't allow yourself to be fearful, anxious, or tense."

A gentle choral theme past Krozac's ears and then faded away. "You came from the sky to see me!"

"We descended from the sky to pay our utmost respect to Khandaburro Derwish and to all who served and still serve in this Derwishieland."

"Who he is, pray tell?"

"He is our legend! The landscape before was infested with bad jinn, demons, and drought. This legendary man revived it and exterminated all the bad jinn."

"Who are you, then?"

"We are jinn too, but we are good, plenty good. We are good jinn, we are angels."

A gentle soulful theme past Krozac's ears and then faded out. "We found him dead next to a camel—"

"He died six months, before you arrived here—"

"Did he die alone; and how?"

"They killed him, the bad jinn. We all felt sorrowful about his death."

"But you told me that he eradicated them all."

"He died and they vanished without a trace."

"Is that right?"

"They had a Mount Everest peak of envy toward him, because he was a philanthropist and he was greatly connected to the heavens. They decided to wipe him out in the name of abomination toward any philanthropist and after all toward the sky . . . they were furious when they witnessed what he had accomplished in a brief period of time. They decided to do away with him by using a swirly force; as you know they were invisible bodies . . . they used their swirly spell of force on him. At first, they tricked him into a slowly swirl around himself, then they kept him swirling until the swirl shifted to a higher rate of celerity. Then they increased the invisible swirly force until he became glowing like a solid amethyst. As they were gloating over his suffering, a supernatural glare released from his body engulfed them all in a matter of seconds like a quicksand in the air, and became non-existent. As the swirling force ceased, he dropped dead onto the sandy earth. Thus, the idea of eternal life of the bad jinn had been extinguished for all future time by the late great Khandaburro Derwish."

"I dreamt about him."

"I knew you dreamt about him."

"How did you know I dreamt about him?"

"I rerouted the dream to you."

"I wonder."

"He transpired in your dream as a glowing mass of light in the shape of a person of great stature with a hunchback spinning around himself, while shaking a wooden tambourine."

"I am smothered with wonder from head to foot."

"Do you know why he was shaking a tambourine?"

"No, pray tell, please."

"Bad jinn despise tambourines. A tambourine expels all bad jinn."

"I will take it under consideration."

"The only thing that you're supposed to do is to be faithful until the end of your time; faithful in the small things, like a tambourine."

"Do you think they will return here again?"

"As long as Khandaburro Derwish's grave remains on his land, they will never dare to return back here again. This land is shielded by his soul! Your blood flow, now belongs to his land, and you must not concern about them anymore."

"We feel a bonded kinship with this land."

Zoltar pointed his first finger toward the sky, and said, "That's our home." Then, he asked for a permission to leave.

When the host gave his consent for them to depart, Zoltar and his wife quickly got up and exited from the tent, leaving their maiden daughters behind. Krozac followed them out of his tent, and said, "You are not leaving now, are you?"

"Yes, we must; we thank you for your most kind hospitality."

"What about your daughters?"

"Good people are meant to be with good people."

"That's how the life works."

"The wife is the sacred key of the Derwishieland."

"A good wife makes a good life, but not for one foot in the grave. We are too old, our lives are long over."

"A good man makes a good wife and a good life," said Zoltar. Then suddenly he appeared with white feather angel wings, he added, "I can fly with my wings; and you can fly without wings when you hold on to your dreams."

"Is this real?" Krozac asked.

"Yes, it's real as can be. Real as Khandaburro Derwish's grave."

Krozac was amazed at how the key of reality can turn out to be, he found a woman next to him, woman next to Shug, woman next to Rosco, and a woman next to Bolanos.

Zoltar was assisted by his white-feather angel-wings, gifted his rite of passage, "By the power vested in me by the heavens, I now pronounce you, Krozac and Gwyneth, husband and wife; Shug and Sabrina, husband and wife; Rosco and Dahlia, husband and wife; Bolanos and Angelique, husband and wife," he continued, "our dearest daughters, this is an emotional parting between you and your parents, there is always a limit where things stand and we have to be satisfied that parting is one of the pillars of life." He smiled at each one of his newly sons-in-law. "Oh, my dearest sons-in-law," he said. "There is no doubt at all in my mind that I am fortunate to have you as my sons-in-law; and there is no doubt in the back of my mind you will take loving care of my precious daughters." Then he and his own wife, Zeena, flapped their white-feather angel-wings and flew sky-bound to their home.

The four newly wedded husbands looked upward to the flying angelic beings disappearing into the starry filled sky and then gazed back at their newly wedded wives with bated breaths. They concluded what they had witnessed was from the comprehension of the unexplainable. Each husband took his wife back to his place of residence; and that was where the miracle happened, their tents vanished and was replaced by modest houses. The newlywed's homes were clay houses equipped with a bedroom, kitchen and a bathroom. Their new wives told their new husbands that this was a gift granted from the heavens.

The four men were ascetic in the temptations of life, including women—they had never been wed before. The four young women had lived their brief lives in the sky with chaste. Since that chanted night, they became beloved married couples: seventy-five-year-old Krozac and Gwyneth; seventy-three-year-old Shug and Sabrina; seventy-two-year-old Rosco and Dahlia; seventy-year-old Bolanos and Angelique.

At the dawn of the next morning they heard jingling musical sounds coming from outside of their honeymoon havens. The four men rushed from their homes to examine what they had just heard; they observed four of the same tambourines dangling in the mid-air and rattling all by themselves, without any visible signs of human interaction. The quadruplet of tambourines slowly began to drift away while the men were intensely curious of pursuing them. When the tambourines approached a high clay wall, they made a thunderous silvery rings for a brief matter of seconds then vanished into thin air. The men recognized the sacred setting the moment they laid their eyes upon it—Khandaburro's tomb was surrounded by a high clay wall. They entered the tranquil site to discover Khandaburro's tomb was covered by an emerald green silk cloth with the four matching silent tambourines were displayed upon his sacred tomb. All at once, each of them grabbed a tambourine, grasping it in one hand and striking it with the other hand, while dancing in unison around Khandaburro's tomb and chanting: "O Heaven, descend on the grave of beloved Khandaburro Derwish with your light and might, keep his place in its sacred space, bless his soul and his role of this land."

From that moment on, the lives of the four married men had suddenly changed as they transformed into hermits and practiced asceticism life-styles. They were leaving their homes twice a day, once at noon and again at the stroke of midnight, to the clay wall that surrounded Khandaburro's tomb. People observed them as they were dancing around the wall, beating their tambourines and chanting: "O our Khandaburro Derwish, forgive all the sins and bad deeds on your Derwishieland, until we join you and in the hereafter. O Khandaburro Derwish."

It has been told that they lived on that land for a few memorable years, probably seven years in all. In that brief period of time of their lives, their fertile fields flourished with its annual-abundant crops of fruits and vegetables. The livestock of camels, sheep and goats also flourished during those years. They were the original band of caretakers who looked after the trade with the caravans; and the business kept a steady uphill pace for a prosperous growth in that area. And it has been said that the good Jinn provided the Derwishieland with more simple buildings and unpaved primitive roads.

Something inexplicable occurred after their marriages. The time literally reversed the hands of the clock for the men, whereas the time stood still for the wives. Without clear rules of the land, the men were regressing back to their younger days, as every year of their lives reverses ten years back, while their youthful wives were blessed with the secret of springtime gift of the fountain of youth. They lived as husbands and wives for five years; no one can be certain if they had offspring, but if they had children, they were certainly invisible. The four men shrank in age and body shape until they returned back to the stages of toddlers and babies, and finally heaven sealed their fate and they followed one after another. First, Bolanos died at the age of five months; second, Rosco died at the age of one year; third, Shug died at the age of two years; and fourth and the last, Krozac died at the age of three years. They were buried next to Khandaburro Derwish's tomb with marked graves as follows: here lies Bolanos Derwish, here lies Rosco Derwish, here lies Shug Derwish, and here lies Krozac Derwish. The band of sisters supported one another to the end, and when they all became widows, the sky beckoned them back, and they obeyed.

There is a problematic belief, some people believe that Khandaburro Derwish descended from heaven to restore the earth and those upon it, and many of them believe in his abilities to heal man's intractable psychological and physical diseases. But a vast number of people regard Khandaburro Derwish as the Godfather of the Derwishes, who inspired his faithful followers with his spirit and they promoted it, while others regard him as a fictional character. There are people that believe of paying tribute to his tomb or even visit his land will protect them from the plights in life and open them for the ways of delights. No matter how many interpretations about Khandaburro Derwish's character, he remains an adoring myth and he will remain in people's minds-and-hearts until heaven inherits the earth once again and those among it.

The Trip

The following events took place in mid-spring of 1965, in a city named Addahra. In that city lived a family of six. They resided in an apartment of a three-story building—each storey had one apartment. They occupied the middle, second, floor, while other two Italian families were residing in the ground and third floor. The four-room apartment was commodious enough for Jonah Kadprist, the head of the family; Lima Ryan who kept her maiden name, a housewife; and their four young sons: Kareem, Joseph, Freddie, and Lute; sixteen, fifteen, nine, and seven years old, respectively. Kareem stood at 6-foot tall, slim built, with a brawny physical structure. He had a black hair, dapper style, and dark brownish eyes. Kareem usually dressed like all other teenage boys of his peer group—blue denim jeans, T-shirt, and sneakers without socks. He was a strong silent type, for a young man of sixteen. Kareem had a charismatic persona, who found it easy to attract attractive girls out of their doors. When he was younger, he tripped and fell down a flight of stairs which left him permanently with a distinctive scar on the top right-side of his forehead.

His sixty-one-year-old father, Jonah; and his thirty-eight-year-old mother, Lima; were completely two different individuals and their ships had already sailed for them ever to change. There was a vast difference in age between them; she was twenty-three years younger. He was six feet two inches tall, well built, with a short grey hair; she was five feet two inches tall, clean-limbed, with black short pixie hairstyle. They were different even in their clothing styles, he had one dress code; and she had no dress code. He wore loose cotton white shirts upon his white trousers with a white cloak, and a flat brimless white cap over his head. She wore different types of brightly colored dresses with no veils.

His father was a moderate man, but his mother was a strong-willed woman.

Kareem received his driving licence when he was just sixteen. Passing the driving test the first time around was an ecstatic achievement for young Kareem, and it was grand news to all of the family, except his father, Jonah. Even the air circulating around their household was in very good spirits, and as quick as a jack-flash, the air flew the news from their home and spread it to the entire neighborhood. The household and the neighborhood were pulsed with the positive vibrations of Kareem's new driving licence accomplishment. Gradually, herds of women and children drifted in through the revolving front door of their home to shake the hand of his mother, Lima, in congratulation. His father had no congratulators; he remained quiet for few days, allowing himself to cogitate about what the next step would be.

The next morning, as the sun rose bright and balmy, Kareem awoke with joyful hope in his heart, hoping to hit the wheel of the car jackpot. He came out from his bedroom around seven o'clock and came close just enough to eavesdrop on his parents conversation in the kitchen.

In the morning, Lima and Jonah sat at the kitchen table and drank their favorite blend of coffee, while discussing their plans for the day, until the car issue resurfaced again. "Jonah, when are going to purchase the car?" she asked. The expression on her face reflected both an answer and demand.

Jonah looked uncomfortable, and hesitated a moment before answering. "I am in no mood to talk about the car, now." That was the end of the conversation for that particular morning.

There were quite a few teenagers in the neighborhood who constantly were questioning-pestering Kareem, about when he ever will drive his own car, and when his dad was going to buy him a car. The pressure was way too much for Kareem to handle, as he had no answer for their repetitive hounding questions. He passed the pressure from the local inquisitive teenagers on to his mother, in return to find a solution to this transportation dilemma. His mother was comforting him, by saying: "I'm just waiting for the right moment to talk with your dad. Don't worry; everything will be fine, everything will work out fine."

One day Lima broke the ice-tray of the tense silence, and said, "Now look here, Jonah, I know you have a ton of money hoarding away in several of your secretive treasure chests and you own quite few properties, which I don't even know about and where you've hidden them all away. You always hide everything from me; you treat me as if I'm your foe—"

"I don't trust you with my money, because you are a serious lesion to my financial business," said Jonah.

"Don't you dare call me a lesion; it wasn't my choice to marry an old man like you, in the first place. I will never forgive my late father as long as I have a breath left in me, that he forced me to marry up with the likes of you, when I was only sixteen." Then in Italian: "*Capisci?* Do you understand?"

"Don't mess with me, Lima, or—"

"Aha, or what?"

"Or, I'll divorce you."

"Hurrah, yippee; what a liberating day that would be; let me tell you, a thing or two, I despised you from the first instant I laid my naïve and silent eyes upon you, on that black day of long ago. Is that enough or do you want me to open my mouth and spill out all the hateful beans? Just go ahead with your divorcing joke of a threat, and make it real for me if you are a real man."

"Trust me! It's going to happen—"

"Hurry up, hurry up—"

"Okay, divorce-minded wife."

"I'm satisfied with the muddle of my misery, but the misery doesn't want to satisfy me." Her voice sounded so serious and sad that silenced him at once.

Without speaking another word to her, he provided her with a strange stare, while his face was distorting with flare; then he slammed the front door behind him. He hurried across the floors of the house in a state of great rage, in the home of his mother, Merriam. A melancholy mixture of pain and sadness filled the house, days after he left; and the hope for getting Kareem a car soon dwindled away.

One day Kareem visited with his Grandmother Merriam and said that he hoped that his father would return back to their family home. His youthful words blended sweetly with her aged mind, and said, "Your father will return soon back to his home."

Two weeks later, Jonah finally showed up back home. He displayed some signs of flexibility with the negotiation about the car—he had more of a positive attitude than previously expressed.

As he was walking down the hall, she triggered his presence in the house. She came out from her bedroom and stood quietly for a moment, then came closer to him, and said, "How is the bivouac with your mother?"

"There's no place like home," Jonah said.

"Really—"

"For sure, there isn't."

"Could be—"

"Let's bury our harmful hatchet!"

She glared up at him, and said, "When are going to buy him that car?"

He said with an affable voice, "This month I will buy him a car, you can bank on it."

"Not this month; not this week; not even the day after. You buy him a car tomorrow, not one second after. Is that clear?"

"It's crystal clear like a chandelier." Finally he conceded to her demand, without any resistance.

Somehow, next day, Kareem managed to present a used yellow Volkswagen to his dad. He needed his stamp of approval, and consequently of the first order of business his 2000 dollars for the car.

Everyone (Lima, Joseph, Freddie, and Lute) crowded to one of the living room bay window, admiring the German auto and were so supportive except for Jonah. He wasn't in the mood to buy a used car; he kept himself in the living room, listening to the afternoon broadcast, on the console radio. As for Kareem, he found himself in front of his father in the living room. "Dad, the car is downstairs in front of our building, here and now."

His father turned off the radio just as Kareem entered the living room, and said, "How on earth did you bring me a used car to buy, just like that. Are you kidding?"

"I wish I was."

"Then—"

"Relax Dad, the car is only one year old, and in good shape with low mileage, the car has new tires, I really want to have this car."

"Well, if I am going to buy a car; it's going to be a family car not your own set of wheels."

"Okay Dad . . . trust me, the car is good as new—"

"Nonsense. Stop acting like any regular schmo on the street! I need to know the con man who stuffed your noggin full of week old bologna. All used cars are at high risk of being on the dicey side and nothing on this planet can fool me about con game of dicey cars."

The presence of his mother interrupted their conversation. "Don't be such a wet blanket, Jonah! I have a solution that might work. What about our Italian neighbors, downstairs, Francesco? His wife, Giulia, told me, that he knows plenty about cars. Let him check-out the car first then we'll decide, huh?"

"Okay, if that's the way you want it, so be it."

As soon as Kareem heard his father's grant the green light, he ran out from the living room and contacted Francesco Morelli about checking the car. Francesco took the car out for a test spin, drove it around the neighborhood and back; then he got out of the car quite displeased. He looked directly at Kareem, and said, "*Roba vecchia*. Garbage."

Kareem said, "*Cos c'e di sbagliato con la macchina?* What is wrong with the car?"

"*Mi dispiace. La macchina non prende la velocita*. I am sorry. The car doesn't take the speed."

"*Grazie molto, Signore Morelli*. Thank you very much, Mr. Morelli."

"*Prego*. You're welcome." Without speaking another word to Kareem or Nino, the car owner; Francesco Morelli returned to his home.

"What did he tell you about the car?" Nino said to Kareem.

"I don't know what I'm going to say to my father?" said Kareem.

"Say what?"

"Francesco said, 'The engine is no good.'"

Nino then pointed his middle finger at Francesco's apartment, and said, "*Figlio di puttana*. Son of a bitch." Then he shook his head in a stage of rage, as he was spinning off, putting the pedal to the metal.

After the failed tale of the yellow VW Beetle, the alarm siren sounded off for a new car. One afternoon during the same week, Jonah bought a new car for the family—it was a white Volkswagen Beetle. He had paid 6000 US dollars for the car and informed Lima that a family road trip is required first to the Land of Derwishes to bless the new family car.

For the first time in their young tender-footed lives, the kids heard their father's voice speaking impulsively about the derwishes. None of the kids had a single clue what the derwishes even looked like? And why they call them the derwishes? Their mother did some first-hand Nancy Drew detective work of her own, for information about the derwishes for her husband. She had zero satisfaction to satisfy her innate desire in any "Blessings from the derwishes"; somewhere in the back of her sceptical mind she didn't buy into them. Jonah knew there was overwhelmingly reason of truth to what his wife felt. Actually, the only fact that he was aware of, was about a holy man named Khandaburro Derwish who lived and died in a village, years ago. After his untimely death, a band of his followers—which named themselves the "derwishes"—built a showcase like shrine surrounding his gravesite. Since that time, the village was known by the "Derwishieland" and a slogan for good fortune. Since then, people flocked to his shrine from all parts of the country, seeking his blessing; and to seek cures for their physical, mental and spiritual impairments. The derwishes became the inherited gatekeepers of the shrine believed in his array of magical powers; and subsequently became his loyal servants with full power over the stream of visitors to his shrine.

The day soon arrived, when the family was to depart for their adventure to the Land of Derwishes—it was on a Thursday of the second week after the school vacation was in full gear. The kids were awoken by the sunlight glittering through the apartment windowpanes, around six o'clock in the morning. With glowing grins from their anticipation of the family road trip, the kids had no desire for breakfast that particular morning, despite the fresh coffee aroma which was filtering from the kitchen. They asked their parents for permission to get ready, and when they got the green light from their mother, they ran like racehorses through the starting gate, toward their bedrooms. They left their parents in the kitchen—the father was listening to the morning news on the radio at six o'clock while drinking a cup of coffee with his wife. The children dressed in their finest attire then carried their one medium-sized shared suitcase to the new car. They held their breaths while waiting a half hour of eternity for their parents to join them. When they arrived, Jonah took his position on the front passenger seat next to driver seat; while Lima, Joseph, Freddie, and Lute took refuge on the back bench seat. Finally, when everything-everyone was ready for take-off, Kareem gripped the steering wheel, as he was propelling the new family car for its first maiden voyage through the bustling city streets.

The Derwishieland was nearly three hundred miles in distance. It was a warm and sunny day for their family road trip. The morning sea air carried a mild-breeze with a lingering faint scent with a salty taste. Since it was a warm summer day, Lima told Kareem to stop at any small restaurant or soda shop before heading out of town. Everyone agreed to the delightful idea of the cool refreshments before hitting the long dry trail. Kareem reversed the car from the pavement of the family apartment building, and then began to drive between two-story buildings toward a nearby shop. Without speaking, Kareem went to a shop and brought back a variety of soft drinks in icy-cold bottles for everyone. By the time they began to take sips from their drinks, the car started to head out from the city heading to the Land of Derwishes.

The road was fairly straight, with occasional rough patches filled with landmine-sized potholes; one that had been worn out over a period of years. At some stretches of the road, it resembled a rough dark flowing river that drifts a raft so awkwardly along its course. The roadway was barely wide enough for one car to travel in each direction; and there were no white or yellow lines running down the median strip of the rural roadway. The shoulders of the byway were lined with dust from the endless miles of desert landscape with an assortment of hazardous loose gravel. There were utility poles and few billboards advertising for the derwishes along the route of the byway. The dromedaries (one-humped camels), sheep and goats that were accompanied by herders, shepherds, and goatherds along the way, were evermore remained so like a vast array of painted portraits.

Suddenly a camel appeared out of the blue in the middle of the byway, as if it was a local hitchhiker thumbing for a ride. Kareem braked the car in the middle of the byway as he was at his wits' end.

"Kareem, move the car at once and just pull over here, very quickly right now and stop the car. We'll see if the camel will clear off soon," Jonah said. He signaled him to pull over.

As soon as he heard his father's order, Kareem quickly drove the car to the side of the road and parked there. "Oops, there is another car behind us, now," he said.

"It looks like we are caught between the sap and the bark," Lima said. Then, turning her eyes toward the camel, she added, "Looks like the camel is coming from the derwishes' straitjackets welcoming party."

"Nip it in the bud, Lima," said Jonah.

The youngsters were amused by the sudden sighting of the camel, which reminded them of the cartoons about camels in their comic books. They wished to view a genuine-live camel someday—and this was the day one of their childhood wishes became true.

"Whoa, this is a real camel; it looks more fascinating than in the comic book versions. Mister Camel is tall as a palm tree and as huge as a city bus," said Joseph.

"No dinging around my boy, you are looking at the real show," said

Jonah. He reassured everyone by explaining that a camel could do no harm except if it wished to.

"What are they useful for?"

"They provide us with milk, meat and textiles. Also, a camel is well known as a 'ship of the desert' it can walk and survive long dry periods in the desert."

All of a sudden, a man appeared from behind a bush near the camel. The man was carrying a long spear like a stick, and as swiftly as a machete thrower he threw the big stick toward the camel. The camel caught the deadly stick in its mouth, and began to chase after him. The man was running like a panicky fat jackrabbit in front of a hungry determined fox. After a cat and mouse game and high-speed chase, the camel thrust the captured prey down on the scorched desert sand with its long muscular legs. Miraculously, the man managed to escape from the long-heavy legs of the camel, and began to run for his life. The camel immediately raced after the man while he was running like a targeted hunted deer. When it reached him, it started kicking him forward by its massive legs, and biting him on the top of his head like a ripen apple by its razor lengthy-frontal-teeth. The camel then swung his head at the man, and violently kicked him at the same time; then it took a powder leaving behind its victim lying in a pool of blood on his death bed of sand. Both the camel's large leathery feet pads and the man's feet left a cloud of sandy dust in the aftermath of the bloodbath.

It was turning out to be a bad omen, all the way around. The grisly scene of a camel attacking a man formed a high degree state of anxiety for the entire family; which embedded in their memories from that day forward.

Lima sighed deeply, then leaned over to Jonah, and said, "This is a sign to return back home at once. These are the signs from the skies! We can't afford to let our guard down; allowing something else much more horrific to occur, if we don't take heed to the signs."

Jonah looked back at Lima, "Returning back because of this, uh-uh. We are continuing our trip to the Land of Derwishes. We are going there right now!" He glanced at Kareem. "Let's go, you did good driving this morning," he told his son once.

Kareem nodded agreeably, "Thank you, sir." He started the engine. "Yes, sir," he said. "Let's go, then."

"That's a boy."

She glared hard through the back passenger side window, while passing through the scene where the camel attacked the man. "Jonah," she began worriedly, "Jonah, you going to stop to check the man out if he needs help, won't you?"

"I don't reckon," said Jonah.

"Oh, you don't, huh?"

"No, I don't. I don't want to interfere between the man and the camel. Can't you see; it's a payback day for the man."

"What do you mean by a 'payback day' huh?"

"Since the beginning of time, what goes around comes around . . . when misdeeds must be punished."

"What did he do to deserve all this brutality by a wicked creature?"

"I don't know what he did or what he didn't do and if the man was good news or bad news to the camel. But I know that a camel is a revenge-minded kind of animal. It is always itching for a kill if you mistreat it. You follow me?"

She expressed back with a blank expression when he told her of his knowledge of camels. "You know, huh?" she lowered her voice to a whisper, "you are just a real camel whiz, Jonah. I guess that figures."

As the car was traveling along the two-way road, the family was enjoying the tranquil scenes of some homesteads (small farmhouses surrounded by land), cactuses, and date palm trees overlooking the roadway. They were entertained by a pair of red-tailed hawks which flew above them forming perfect circles in the sunny-summer blue sky. The game plan was to drive to a local diner on the way and get a bite to eat, and then hit the road to the Derwishieland. After several miles, an aged sign with white printing on a black background, read "Good Eats and Sweet Treats (ten miles ahead)" and appeared to have no competitive companion challenging it along the roadway.

Right before they reached the diner, they approached an older car model with flat front tire was parked on the side of the road. "Are we going to stop, this time?" Lima said.

"You seriously want us to stop!" Jonah said.

"Why not, then?" she asked sincerely.

Jonah shook his head, and said, "Seriously, I don't think so. It could be a setup for a trap. It's risky and dangerous spin on a roulette wheel and could be a planned surprise attack, who knows? We don't want to take that chance. No." He looked at Kareem. "Keep going, son, and don't stop."

"All right, then," Kareem said. He pressed his right foot on the accelerator and sped off.

"No speed. Is that plain enough?" his dad said soberly.

He eased his right foot off the accelerator pedal. "That's plain enough for me." He drove with even more caution, allowing the accelerator pedal to slow the car—fifty miles per hour.

After fifteen minutes of driving, they arrived at the "Good Eats and Sweet Treats" Diner. Luckily, there was a gas station next door to the diner. Kareem parked the car at one of the gas pumps and filled it up, then parked the car next to the side of the diner, while his dad was paying for the gas; and then they all trailed inside the diner. The sweet smell of fried chicken was the only smell lingering in the diner. The diner was roasting and completely empty of any customers, except for one short pudgy bald-headed man who was the proprietor of the diner. He introduced himself as "Piccoly" and has owned the place for nine years. The middle-aged Piccoly had an abnormally beady set eyes jiggling behind his black round thick lens glasses. He was dressed in a shabby outfit—long clown looking whitish pants and a short-sleeved whitey shirt that revealed his hairy assorted tattooed blubber-arms. He walked with a bow legged gait, like he was infested with rickets; and he was trudging with a rustling vibration over the floor of the diner as his soles were trampling on the floor by his worn out brownish sandals. Apparently, he was the only one who prepares the grub, serves it up to his customers—the chubby owner was a real jack of all trades. There were two small wooden tables seating four that was located by the side of the wall. On the wall above them was a wall-mounted board—read, "Derwishes are in the air and their souvenirs for sale" beside a small and limited menu board. There were a variety of clay figurines (small statues) that represent the popular derwishes figures in a glass display case, next to the cash register on the front counter.

They settled for fried eggs and cheese sandwiches, milk, and bottles of water to take with them. Jonah paid for the food and drinks as the entire family were just getting ready to leave the diner.

"Yo," Piccoly's raspy voice called out, while the family were departing from the diner. "A derwish figurine is a real good luck charm for your trip. Why don't you come back in, mister, and buy one for your happy family?"

"Might I enquire about the statuettes?" asked Jonah.

"Go on, then."

"You're a potter, aren't you?"

"I could not make them derwishes. I wish I had, but I am no potter."

"Who makes them?"

"You better sit way back, this one give ya a real jolt."

"I am here, not much, but I'm still here"

"Nobody makes them derwishes. The stork delivers them to me."

"I will be dogged! What kind of crack is that?"

"It is no joke; on my word as a gentleman."

"You are fascinated with them figurines, aren't you?"

"I'm not fascinated with them figurines none; I am fascinated only by them derwishes. The derwishes have always held a fascination for me."

"There you are. . . I have to give it some thought."

Piccoly then waved with his hand as he was smirking at them, "Come back any old time, mister." Then, he waved with both his grubby-greasy paws above his shining bowling bald head and got no attention. "Be seeing you, guys" he said. "See you later!" He stood up, wobbled, and then went back to his con diner routine.

"The later; the better," Jonah said with a relieved voice.

Lima whispered, "You fat old coot; once a coot always a coot." Then, turned to Jonah, she added, "He's no more than a typical carnival flimflammer! We better get the hell out of this dump, before I completely lose it on him. He is as crooked as a three dollar bill."

"He's selling more than food in there; besides his hot air; he is up to no good. Come on, let's get out of this neck of the woods," Jonah said.

After they left the diner, they went inside the car. Everyone was unusually famished, except Lima. She distrusted and disliked Piccoly at first sight, as much as she was wary of consuming his concoction of sandwiches.

She muttered nervously, "Money brings food, but not appetite." She extended her right hand. "Please Jonah," she said. "Hand me those greasy sandwiches, please."

Jonah handed her one sandwich, and said, "Let's eat before hitting back on the road, huh?"

"I don't want a sandwich, I want all the sandwiches. Don't eat any, and give them all to me, hurry please."

He handed her all the sandwiches in the paper bag, and said, "What are you going to do with all these sandwiches?"

She took the paper bag from her husband, and placed it on her lap. "Let me try to catch my breath first and I'll just show you what I'm going to do." She tapped nervously on Kareem's shoulder. "Kid, you drive now and focus your attention on the road. Go on, then; go on, then," she said.

As the car was once again en route to the derwishes homeland, the children were neither quiet nor happy after their mother apparently seized the sandwiches for herself. Joseph, Freddie, and Lute began to scream in ear-splitting volume at their mother; demanding an explanation, why she flatly refused to let them have their long overdue lunch. Kareem kept focused on two things at the same time—on his driving and on the road ahead—and his father remained silent—did not utter a single word—and Kareem followed his lead.

All at once, Lima lowered the rear right-side car window and threw out the greasy paper bag containing all the sandwiches on the side of the road, without seeding doubt in her mind. As she was tossing out the sandwiches, her voice followed them, "Good riddance. Mother Nature will claim them in her own time as she does every time."

"Why did you throw away the sandwiches, Mama?" said Joseph, while Freddie and Lute were crying in pools of non-stop tears for food.

"A dipshit, like Piccoly is pitiful peddler for his sandwiches."

Jonah spoke slowly and distinctly in a supportive tone to his wife and children, "It is not the end of the world, is it? Your mother is right. We don't want to get sick from eating those sandwiches, do we?" He leaned his head backward and winked in reassurance at his children. "Hey, boys, we don't need any old tummy ache, do we? Surely, we don't. But we would if we had eaten the sandwiches, not much doubt about that," he said. "Keep your bright eyes fixed for another roadside diner, huh?"

The kids babbled simultaneously, "Okay, Daddy."

"Well, then, that's settled," said Lima.

The soft sound of the new engine began to escort the car through the sunlit afternoon road once more. There was sparse skittering of sand on the shoulders and across the blacktop road, stirred by a whispered breath of a summer afternoon warm breeze, and an infrequent vehicle. As the sun rose bright and balmy; the afternoon sky was without a single cloud, the car began to warm up rapidly—enough for everyone to feel the sizzling afternoon temperature and smell of the creosote bushes (likened to the smell of tar). Both Lute and Freddie cried themselves into a much-needed nap on their mother's lap; while Joseph was peeking across the vast desert horizon, as if he was waiting for a diner to magically appear from nowhere. Kareem was so alert and in control as never before—that was his first taste of driving the new family car—he kept his eyes constantly on the road; while his father and mother were closely observing their first-born son like a pair of hawks, during his inaugural driving of the family's new car, on the family road trip.

While driving at a leisurely pace of one mile after another, Kareem continued to drive and survey the desert roadway in total quietude. There was about an hour left of driving toward the derwishes homeland, when he witnessed an unusual site in his teenaged world—something mystifying loomed on the horizon. "Dad, there is a standing water like a river crossing the road ahead. I can't cross that river by driving across it."

"First, there are no rivers in the desert; second, what you're seeing is a water-like image on the ground, it is not a real water, it's a mock-up version of water—" his father said.

Kareem seemed bewildered, "What shall I do?"

"Keep on driving, Kareem, and you will see for yourself; as you keep approaching the water-forming image, you will see the water disappears and appears in another place. It's referred to as a 'desert mirage.'"

"What does mirage mean?"

"Means 'to look at water in the desert when it is not there'; it's a fiction, but it's true."

"I don't understand how it could be real and not real at the same time?"

"Well, Kareem, you see a pool of water from a distance and the water shape moves away as you approach it. In fact there is no water at all out there. The water is a just an illusion, not real."

"I can barely wrap my head around this."

Jonah rubbed his sagacious chin thoughtfully while he was focusing at the mirage floating gently on the road, "The sun rays seemed to bend when entering the sweltering air layers, and teases us with a false image. Got it . . . keep quiet now and keep your eyes peeled on the road while you're driving." He leaned his head back. "Hey Joe," he said. "How's our first mate in the backseat crow's nest doing?"

"Still watching over the lookout, Dad," said Joseph.

"That's good enough for all of us," his dad said. "A mirage 'false water' is a natural phenomenon, based on deception to trick the parched inhabitants of the desert into believing in it and finding it. It is nothing more than an illusion of seeing water over hot surfaces." The reliable humming sound of the new tires against the afternoon heated asphalt kept the car advancing toward the entrance of the derwishes homeland, without crossing any standing water.

Around two o'clock in the afternoon, and after seven gruelling hours of driving, they finally reached their destination, the homeland of the derwishes. There was an old wooden signage, black background with bold white lettering, hanging above the entrance of the village, which read "Welcome to Derwishieland" as a personal gesture of a greeting sign by the founding father of the derwishes to all of his regular-new visitors.

The village of the derwishes was built on a flatland with houses, a grocery store, gift shop, bakery, butcher shop, and a small village inn named Khandaburro Inn. All of the houses were clustered with narrow soil paths running between them, often reserved for pedestrians. The houses were built with the same and simple design, low and wide with one main door and two windows with matching shutters on both sides. Some houses were newer, some were older, and some were dilapidated. The exterior walls of the houses were painted pure white, and the wooden doors and the windows were painted in many shades of green. At the center of the village on the main road, there was a grocery store with its display racks full of tomatoes, onions, cucumbers, watermelons, and prickly pears; a souvenir shop with its windows brimming with an assortment of figurines and folklore items of the derwishes; a bakery, with tantalizing aromas of fresh baked breads, cookies, cakes and their renowned derwish cream puffs of a buttery flavor circulating in the air; a butcher shop showcasing bloody sections of meats and plucked chickens hanging upside down on meat hooks outside the shop. There was an open market two blocks away from the butcher shop. The baaing sheep with their foul smells were drifting in annoyance through the village air outside their barbed wire market.

The men's costumes were similar style across the entire village. The outfits consist of a knee-length baggy white tunic shirts; baggy white pants with elastic waistband; white skull cap; and rubber slippers. As for the village women, the clothes consist of a silky colored blouse with bishop sleeves, embroidered with beads; ankle-length white baggy trousers with elastic bands; bright matching embellished scarf with brightly reddish pom-poms; and leather sandals. It was a customary for a woman in the village to wear a string of imitation pearls dangling from her neck down in front of her chest. The youngsters of the village wore a standard garment; white pants, lightweight long-sleeve shirts, sandals, and brimmed hats for the boys and multi-colored scarves for the girls, around their heads.

They were greeted at the front entrance of the Khandaburro Inn by a tall doorman in his thirties; he was wearing an ankle-length white garment, with a matching white skull cap, and white slippers. His face was tan, and it provided a clue of welcoming guests. On cue he opened the front passenger car door, and said gleefully, "Welcome to the Land of the Derwishes, sir; and be our welcomed guests, sir. Thor is at your beck and call, sir."

"Thank you, Thor," Jonah said.

"How was the drive, sir?"

"It couldn't be better."

"Be over the moon about the derwishes, sir; and everything will be dandy, sir." Then, he took their luggage, and said, "Follow me, please, sir."

With loving care, the father cradled the sleepy Freddie in his robust arms, and the mother followed the same lead for the sleepy little Lute; while the weary Joseph was leaning slightly like the Tower of Pisa against his brother, Kareem. Even as tired as they were, their tired legs were obediently following the doorman, hoping against hope, that there would be appetizing food and comfy beds waiting for them inside the inn. Thor pushed the main entrance door with his right hand, leaving the door open for the family to enter the inn, and leaving the smell of the stale cooking aromas to be the first host greeting them at the main entrance. The hallway was painted in a warm tone of emerald green and there was luggage and various items on the uneven dirt floor. They walked with extreme fatigue into the warmth of the hallway, and then suddenly Jonah stopped, peering through the cooking aromas, and said, "Where is the front desk located for checking in, Thor?"

"There is no checking in or out in this place, sir; and you don't need to sign anything, sir," continued Thor, "mind the stairs and follow me, sir." He escorted them to an apartment and then unlocked the door. "This is it," he said. "Here we are, accommodation five is for you and your blessed family, sir. May I have your name, please, sir?"

"My name is Jonah Kadprist."

"Here is the key Mr. Kadprist; enjoy—"

Jonah took the key in his hand and took a deep breath. "Is there any food service here?"

"There isn't, Mr. Kadprist."

"How could it be?"

"We provide complete room service. All of the food here is happily prepared by the derwishes; and we will deliver you our most popular dish 'Bazin Pillar of Khandaburro' to you and your family, this evening."

"All right then; we need to have some cold water first." He took out some paper money from his billfold and handed it to Thor.

Thor eagerly grabbed the bills with his right hand while his left hand stretched out to his cap, and in a synchronized motion, his left hand raised the cap while his right hand placed the bills like feathers over his hairless scalp, and then he lowered the cap on his shaven head leaving the money trapped and secured between his skullcap and the cap. "Thankee, Mr. Kadprist. Is there anything also, you want?"

"Cold water and food; and that's the gist of it for now."

"We are the derwishes, when we move we move fast and when we move just watch our smoke."

"You are good man, Thor."

"Sure, real good." He removed his cap and started bowing in front of Jonah, while the bills were flowing from his head like the ripe autumn leaves to the floor. His face was flushed with bright red tone, and gazed away while Jonah was closing the door softly, to avoid him from being embarrassed. Then he quickly snatched the banknotes one by one and retrieved all of them in his hand, while the white cap returned to its perch, on top of his soft-smooth head; then retreated backwards without looking up.

With a sly quick glance over her left shoulder, targeting it for Thor who was outside the closed door, Lima muttered in Italian, "*Non mangero alcun cibo qui.* I am not going to eat any food here."

The apartment was a shabby, down-at-the-heel sort of place. It had two dreary bedrooms, a dingy front room and a limited bathroom; and without a kitchen. There was an old rusted wooden table, in the middle of the front room, with a set of chipped plates, mixed-matched cutleries, and tin cups. There was no real bedroom furniture, except for a set of foam mattresses scattered about over vintage braided multi-colored rugs. The bathroom had no bathtub, no shower either; the only fixture in the so-called bathroom was a wall mounted metal hand sink and a primitive squat latrine. The parents sounded really down and disconsolate as the dwelling was barely hospitable; and moreover, the ground level cooking aromas which filtered in through the closed front room window was entwining with the warm air everywhere inside and outside the apartment.

The exact date of construction of the inn was a mystery; and who built it remains a mystery, too; nevertheless it was likely built by the good Jinn in the late 1800s. The construction within the inn was of stone. The 6000 square foot inn was built as the shape of a fort and the two storey gray walls were designed to tilt toward the inside of the building. The windowless fortress had one roundish top solid green aged wood door; next to it a wooden sign with white text, which read, "Welcome to Khandaburro Inn" on a green background. The building contained a roofless ground floor and one floor which accessed through two staircases by the interior panel sides from the ground floor. There were three narrow prolonged corridors, which furnished with ornate wooden railings, overlooking the open ground hall. The building featured nine apartments, ranging from two-three bedrooms, spaced about the three corridors, reserved only for the seasonal guests.

As was said before, "Sleep is the master and we are his heavy-eyed servants"; sleep turned off their heads which were inflamed by fatigue and exhaustion, and they all immediately exited off to a catnap land, regardless of the dire conditions of the apartment. They slept on foam mattresses which were scattered around the bedroom for one solid hour. Joseph dreamt that someone was banging his noggin, and when he woke up, he heard banging on the apartment door. He jumped quickly yet lightly to his dad, and said, "Dad, wake up, Dad, somebody is knocking on the door, or on the windowpane."

His dad cropped up, and said, "Here we go!"

His mother moaned sleepily, "This is just the beginning of the clown circus!"

When Jonah opened the door; a trio of clown fools flowed inside the apartment like band members in a parade without percussion instruments and shoes as they were announcing the arrival of the evening dinner. They said in one voice, "Dinner time," with a three-fold extension of the letter 'i' in the word 'time'; while Thor was carrying a pitcher of water on his head, one man was carrying a vintage aluminum lidded sauce tureen with ladle on his head, and the other man was carrying an old aluminum lidded tureen on his head. They grabbed their bowls with both hands, and then in a simultaneous movement, lowered them onto the lounge floor; and said simultaneously, "Khandaburro blesses you and Bazin; Bazin Pillar of Khandaburro."

"It does us good to see the food," Jonah said.

"The nightly derwishes show takes aim at nine o'clock, Mr. Kadprist," said Thor.

"Where is that?"

Thor spoke in a tone of enthusiastic optimism, "The show will be here, on the ground floor." He pointed his trigger finger at the corridor. "Oh Khandaburro," he said. "You can watch the show from outside in the corridor."

"Sounds like a real show."

"It will be an insult if you didn't join us."

"Is this your show?"

"It's the derwishes show."

"I can't say anything more against it."

"A basket of blesses, Mr. Kadprist."

"The family will be all together in the corridor to watch the show at nine o'clock." He pulled out a stash of cash from his pocket and gave it to each of them.

Every man received the money, and said, "Thank thee, Mr. Kadprist." They put the money under their awaiting white caps, breezed out backwards, and then the brown-nose Thor closed the apartment door behind him.

One tureen contained a rounded, smooth dome of barley flour dough placed in the middle of the tureen; cooked lamb chops, potatoes, hard-boiled eggs, and hot green chili peppers were arranged around the dome. The other tureen had only one thing—a tomato-based lamb stew. As soon as Jonah lifted the covers of the tureens, the distinctive aroma of fenugreek (maple-syrup-like odor) spread out freely across everyone's nose and mouth. He poured the meat stock over the dome and the rest and then called on each one to the Bazin.

Jonah: Come Lima, and get some food.

Lima: Please, spare me; the smell spoiled my petite appetite. I am not eating one single morsel from this place. Bon appetit!

They gathered around the dish of Bazin, ate a large helping of the food and drank one glass of cold water after another, except Lima who refused to undo her previous stinging words—not be eating one single morsel from this place. They felt fairly heavy-eyed after consuming the food, as it was said, "When one's belly is full, next on the menu is beautiful feeling of dozing-off; sleep is the most beautiful word in the world." That was what actually occurred, they lay on the mattresses asleep with full tummies except for Joseph—he didn't partake in the food, as he was a vegetarian.

Joseph went out swiftly, all by himself, through the corridor and down the stairs to the open ground hall where he detected something strange and out of sync. He saw four greenish double row tambourines with hairy midget size legs with butterfly wings dancing in a circle and rattling like shutters in a wind tunnel. The four prancing tambourines were dancing around a silver-colored censer while dispensing jasmine incense and white fumes in the air. The whimsical movements of the four tambourines were completely self-propelled on autopilot mode. The four tambourines came to an abrupt standstill, only when the white fumes from the incense burner began swirling around itself into the perfect formation of an angel. They circled the censer four times, and each time they stopped, Joseph saw a soft white shape of an angel. When they finished the fifth cycle and stopped, a tall stylized human emerged from the censer in the shape of a gingerbread man and stared at Joseph, like a cat was sizing up a mouse whether to catch it or not.

The seven feet Gingerbread Man had a flat brown body; gigantic circular head with two jack in the box popping rounded white eyes, thick red lips showcasing a sinister big wide smile of a clown; he had no nose, ears, fingers or toes; and he had white squiggly lines across his ample waist, wrists and ankles. He wore a garland of jasmine around his large neck; and one pale yellow jasmine was shouting, "Joseph." He was a cool as a cucumber for a gingerbread man.

A code red alert of fear suddenly swept over Joseph's body; his muscles became stiff, his heartbeat along with his breathing became as if a set of drums were drumming heavily in his eardrums. He soaked in his own sweat, while his silent sounding screams were pouring into the empty well of his chest. Whether consciously or unconsciously, Joseph turned his back on the Gingerbread Man and tried to make a last-ditch escape attempt up the mountainous endless staircase for his father, but the Gingerbread Man's meat hook of a hand was speedier than Joseph's youthful limbs—that was not an even matchup.

Suddenly Joseph felt for his ear as strong fingers were pressing his earlobe and firmly trying to pull him up, he shouted, "Go away, mumbo jumbo."

"Wake up, you hear me; don't let me drag you upstairs by your ear," Jonah said.

"Let me be! I hate you Gingerbread Man! Get lost, drop dead and just let me be."

Jonah muttered nervously, "Mumbo jumbo, gingerbread man; what type of trouble double talk is that! Get up, at once." He yanked Joseph up by his throbbing earlobe. "I raised you better than this," he said. "Little ingrate."

Joseph groggily woke up from his nightmarish of a dream and realized that he had an over-the-top distressed dream. His father tugged him up the staircase from his ever-tender earlobe, while Joseph's tongue was stuttering with only two words, "Sorry, Dad."

Jonah didn't let free of his son's tender earlobe until they both were inside the modest apartment. He instantly locked the apartment door behind him, so no one of the other kids will slip through the door, for another expedition adventure, as Joseph unsuccessfully did.

"Where did you find him? Lima said.

"I found him standing around at the bottom of the stairs," Jonah said. He didn't mention to her that he actually found him sleeping at the bottom of the stairs.

Around nine o'clock that evening, the movement began to circulate in the empty daylight roofless ground floor. The atmosphere was buzzing with an assortment of people and by strong-scented incense which lingered like a waltz in the air. The guests were all summoned by the hubbub as the walls of the first-floor apartments were archaic, just about anyone could hear every syllable of every single word spoken. Furthermore, the smell of food and the scent of the incense began to filter throughout the apartments through the bottom portion cracks of the doorways and some opened/cracked windows. In successive movements, the guests began trickling from their apartments one by one into the corridors; Kadprist Family was among them.

The hall was lit up by four antique light fixtures, each in one corner, allowing the men who squatted down to be visible as the walls were echoing back a mixture of noises. They all sat on different shades of turquoise cushions with their legs just over one another on the lush burgundy carpet. The men were sitting across in opposite groups from one another. Each group consists of six men, with a total of twenty-four men scattered in groups about the four walls. Their heads were covered by non-identical colors of conical headgear; red for the disciples, and black for apprentices. The elder of a high-ranking class within the group wore a crescent star emerald stone attached with his red conical hat which signified the gravestone that would one day stand at the head of his own grave. The men's costumes tended to be similar across the entire hall. It consisted of a lengthy white shirt, long white matching trousers and a black velveteen vest with a set brass buttons displayed on its front. A flowing cardinal red cloak was worn as the outer layer, tied at the right shoulder and the remainder was draped around the body. There was an extra sizeable clay incense burner which was located in the midway of the hall, between the four groups of the derwishes. It flickered with a distant whispered sound of popcorn, while the black charcoal was rapidly being engulfed by flames of fire and puffing out the jasmine scent into the air.

One derwish stood up erect on his tiptoes as a high ranking class derwish, scanning out the nightly regular individuals, to make sure he was fully noticed while he was glancing up toward the spectators, "Good evening and greetings! Every nightfall, we flock in to celebrate the immortal spirit of Khandaburro that once roamed this blessed land and measured as the width of this earth. We beg the Man-Above to make his grave a spacious paradise to inhabit until the day of the Man-Above. He was a mighty set man!" He lifted off his red conical headgear and put it on the floor, revealing his peeled-egg head. "Oh, before I forget let me introduce the derwishes," he said. "We are four bevies of derwishes, as follows: first, bevy of Krozac which led by the high ranking derwish, Fandango; second, bevy of Shug which led by the high ranking derwish, Tarboosh; third, bevy of Rosco which led by the high ranking derwish, Chuka; fourth, bevy of Bolanos which led by the servant of Khandaburro, I, Hopsing." He returned his conical headgear back to his bald head then waved to Fandango, who was just sitting across him.

Fandango stood up next to his group, and said, "If you open yourself to Khandaburro, Khandaburro finds you. The love for him opens the windows to the heart. The love for him opens the flood gates." Then, turning right to Tarboosh who was sitting next to the entrance of the hallway, he added, "I give the floor boards back to you."

Tarboosh rose from his place, and said, "For hundreds of years this land has been held up by bad jinn; Khandaburro Derwish came and kicked the evils real good out of here. Without him you can't have a half of a chance!" He plopped back down in his reserved place.

"Khandaburro Derwish is our ladder; every step we take . . . every step we take is going up; and if you want some calm mixed up with happiness you should look out and keep your eyes and ears open to the derwishes." Chuka said, while he was standing beside his bevy.

Then all the derwishes rose from their places like a pack of hyenas on steroids and began to chant in a repetitive derwish-style chanting with a hodgepodge of not choreographed swaying movements:

"O sweet prayer on
Khan da burro
O sweet prayer on
Khan da burro
Khandaburro is here
He is here and there
O sweet prayer on
Khan da burro
Our night is sweet night
with him and his big site
O sweet prayer on
Khan da burro
We meant him
And we found him
Like our hope chest
And more in his rest
O sweet prayer on
Khan da burro."

Then they sat down simultaneously in their reserved spots, mimicking a well-trained dog act in a low-budget circus.

Besides the Kadprist Family, who their words were stampeded by the laughter; there were many onlookers who were so touched, that some of them were moved to tears—they bought into it.

Lima whispered in Italian, *"Sono idioti*. They are idiots."

"That was real cool, Mom," Joseph said.

"Bunch of crackpots, I would like to punch."

"It looks like we are leaving tomorrow," Kareem said.

"You bet your life we are," Lima said.

As the derwishes were taking an intermission break, Tarboosh stood up in the middle of the hall sizing up the nightly crowd, and said, "I am a palm-reader, a fortune teller. If anyone wants to know the future of his or her lifespan, scroll on down and meet up with me now. And don't forget to bring a nickel with you, and thanks a crunch. A nickel will open the palmistry's eyes to the unseen worlds."

A small number of starry-eyed onlookers descended down the stairs into the hall, including Kareem and his three younger brothers. When Kareem's turn came up, he turned around and pushed his brother, Joseph, face to face with the so-called palm-reader.

"A nickel will open my peepers to your future, my boy. Hand me a nickel, my boy." Tarboosh said. Joseph relinquished the nickel to him without glancing up.

"Good boy, now give me your palm which gave me the nickel," Tarboosh said. He spat a watery liquid out of his bazoo onto Joseph's palm and gently rubbed it in with his right hand. He stared down at Joseph's palm and spent few moments gazing at it, and suddenly his eyes began to beam tidings of good news, he muttered, "What is your name, my boy."

"Yucky," said Joseph.

"Look boy; I am using my eyes now, not my ears. Tell me your name to tell you what I am going to tell you."

"Joseph—"

"How old are you, Joseph?"

"Fifteen years."

"Oh, love sweet fifteen summers! Your sun line is long; you must be some tall midsummers; you know what I'm saying, fifteen summers. And your sun line is high in the sky; you will be some high midsummers; you know what I'm saying, fifteen summers. Love sweet fifteen summers; you know what I'm saying. Your life line is long, too; you know what I'm saying. Where the summers go, you go with the summers; you know what I'm saying. A lucky life is just around the corner of you; you know what I'm saying. Love sweet fifteen summers; you know what I'm saying. " He blew his dripping faucet like schnozzle into his used up kerchief. "Scram, ya, kid; you know what I'm saying." he said. "Go on fifteen summers; you know what I'm saying."

Joseph suddenly realized that he was all alone, everyone left including his three brothers—there were no other children left to be beguiled. He dashed straight upstairs, where his mother was nervously waiting for him.

"Where have you been?" Lima said to Joseph.

"Down in the hall," Joseph said.

"What was his storybook of lies, that goofball?"

"He talked double talk, Mother."

Lima came up, rested her shaky hands on Joseph's innocent shoulders, observing all four of her impressionable children to make certain that her words would be a life-learned-lasting lesson for them in their futures. "I know he is full of hocus-pocus! Oh, how I know that! The future is only destined by the Man-Above and no one else. Tarboosh is just one quack in the pack; don't be taken in by his deceitful bag of tricks, he's nothing but a quack, pure and simple. You must believe only in yourselves, and that's the closed door to unlock the secret key of success. I hope I make myself perfectly clear." Then, turning to Jonah, she added, "I know he beguiled gullible children into giving him their money. I wish I emptied some lead in his empty block of a head."

Jonah did not say anything.

She shook her head, and said in Italian, "*Andiamo a casa.* Let's go home."

"No," Jonah said.

"I don't want to stay one second longer in this three-ring circus—"

"For the sake of the children, let's wait till this show ends; and I'll promise you, we'll leave at sunup tomorrow."

"Will you indeed?"

"I will indeed."

"We want to stay, we want to watch, we want to stay and watch the funny derwishes," the two younger boys pleaded.

Jonah looked at her in the half-light.

"All right then; I stay on one condition: we leave for home at sunup."

"Sunup it is."

She replied in Italian, "*Va bene allora.* All right then."

The two small children romped happily around their mother. "We love you, Mom. We love you, Mom."

"Well, I love you too, so there," Lima said.

All the derwishes stood up in a circle around the Derwish Fandango. They began orbiting in a counterclockwise direction around him, while he was rotating clockwise around himself. They maintained walking with a slow pace around Fandango while he was spinning and spinning, until his pace of spinning began to heat up. Then mysteriously, he disappeared, leaving behind his trademark—his coarse red conical headgear—suspended and spinning in mid-air. When Fandango dematerialized they became dysfunctional—they began whirling, slapping at their foreheads, moaning, and jumping up and down as if a landmine went off underneath their feet. After a while they pulled themselves to their feet and found their way back to their reserved sitting places. Suddenly, the conical headgear disappeared from the mid-air merry-go-round spectacle and re-appeared over the head of an audience member.

Derwish Chuka stood up and began to hunt for the headgear around the hall. He was on pins and needles, hoping beyond hope, to locate it while he was scouting up and down, then stopped suddenly, and said, "Anyone got the headgear of Fandango, he or she can keep it for good luck souvenir."

Unfortunately for the derwishes, the lost conical headgear fell upon Lima's unwelcomed head. Everyone was smirking, giggling, and pointing at her, as if Lima was part of the act in the nightly derwish show. They created a colossal brouhaha over her rave new look with a conical headgear crowning her unwanted head. She was completely outraged with the way that she was treated by the downstairs derwishes and upstairs audience. Angrily, she yanked off the conical headgear from her head and threw it straight back downstairs, and screamed, "How dare you, loathsome drifter!" Then, looking to the viewers, she added in Italian, "*Persone stupide, branco di sciocchi.* Stupid people, bunch of fools."

Jonah and the children trailed Lima while she was walking expeditiously back to the host apartment. The angry Lima slammed the apartment door and glared daggers straight at Jonah, the tattered thread of patience between them began to fade. "I blame you, Jonah, for this entire disastrous trip and especially what has happened to me tonight."

"And you deserve some of the blame as well," Jonah said.

"I have a gut feeling this isn't going to end well!"

"First, nobody held a gun at your head to come on this trip. Second, I told you so many countless times to cover your head, and always you were stuck in one gear—"

"Which gear was I stuck in, huh?"

"You know, the gear 'No.'"

"Keep quiet, and keep your distance from me, I need some overdue beauty sleep."

Jonah nodded in agreement.

The conical headgear fell straight into the incense burner and belched out dense smoke. Chuka looked at the smoke while he was brushing away the tears with his stained sleeve, and said, "I didn't expect the unexpected!"

Joseph's curious mind was tuned to the nightly dramatic uproar; in spite of trying to rein in his adolescence curiosity. He decided to sneak out a second time of the apartment after making sure that everyone was sound asleep despite the importune of the derwishes and their trademark tambourines.

He managed once again the tip-toe show to slip through the apartment door, without being unheard and unobserved; and stood among the audience in front of the wooden corridor railing, viewing down upon the derwishes. The hall was in a state of unrestrained pandemonium, because of the derwishes—they maintained sitting in the cross-legged position, with their heads bobbing in one direction and then in the opposite direction, and banging their hands against the tambourines while chanting wildly without taking a single breath.

Extraordinary events occurred that mysterious night which stained Joseph's mind throughout his entire life as an unforgettable-haunting mystery. A derwish stood up and tilted his flexible head backward—Joseph remained tongue-tied and stoned-cold. He witnessed the derwish was guiding lengthy pieces of nails all the way into his mouth one by one and swallowing them into his gut one after another, like consuming strings of cooked spaghetti. His wide-eyed youthful brown eyes were pinched with fear and mixed with anxiety over the unbelievable performance by the master nail swallower.

The second scene was not less as dangerous than the first one. A barefooted gaunt-looking derwish stood erect and leaped on the flaming tongues of the incense burner. He stood over the fire at least two minutes without being affected by the heat of the burning charcoal, then he jumped to the floor as if nothing had happened to him—his feet didn't burn. Joseph seemed puzzled and felt the heat through his own feet. Another derwish rose up from his place with a glass bottle in his one hand and with a stick in each of his nostril and his ear canal. He stood up, dropping his jaw and began chewing on the glass bottle and swallowing the chewed glass, like he was chewing an ice cube. When he consumed half of the bottle, he threw the other half on the ground and began bouncing his barefoot on the broken glass.

Among the audience clapping, the derwishes rose up at once from their places and began swaying, writhing, chanting, and banging in full throttle against their tambourines. Suddenly, a derwish appeared with a switchblade in his right hand; he stopped and lowered his pants to his groin while grabbing his lower front shirt between his beaver front teeth. He lifted the knife above his bare revealed area—between his groin and belly button—then he began stabbing himself in the lower abdomen with the knife several times. He stabbed himself numerous times without injuries or bleeding a single drop of blood—the scene was a frenzied mayhem.

Joseph felt his left earlobe was dragging him back against his will to the guest apartment— once again he was being dragged by his ear, this time the dragger wasn't his father but his petite mother. "*Viene qui, testa dura.* Come here, stubborn," she said in Italian. Then she dragged him quickly inside the guest apartment and shoved him on the mattress.

She stayed wide awake all night while everyone around her was fast asleep. As the night was entering the homestretch, the hocus-pocus finale spectacle of the derwishes and their unruly audience began to subside. Gradually, the clamor disappeared and was replaced by the cheerful chirping of the birds.

As soon as the downstairs hall suggested the derwishes had already gone home; the family began the returning trip to their home. By sunup the car was running along the bumpy road once again. The family were all eager to be back in their own comfortable homey dwelling. Kareem was very tired, nevertheless he went on driving—he wasn't spoiled, he was a trooper and good driver clean through. Joseph was still in a state of shock for what he witnessed the previous night. The mother remained stoned silent throughout the journey while her two younger boys were dozing away on her lap. As for the father, he directed his attention to his son's driving. Kareem didn't stop at Piccoly's con diner or any other place on the route; he kept driving on through the summer heat as he was instructed by his father. Four hours later, the trip had ended safely, leaving a feeling of omen behind toward the derwishes and the Derwishieland as a whole.

Epilogue

Fandango vowed sweet revenge against the implicated woman who threw his red conical headgear onto the blazing incense burner; following a prolong absence of his trademark headgear. He witnessed it all as he was hiding inside a secret room staring through a cracked window; when he saw it all he was completely thunderstruck and became a kook. There were too many kooks out there, and Fandango was a VIK (a very important kook) member of the Kooky Club.

The summer days careened by with a succession of events, until one early morning when Joseph recognized something was happening between his father and mother. Around five o'clock that morning he heard his parents were arguing and complaining among themselves in their bedroom over some issues that was unclear and vague to him. He looked puzzled for few seconds then decided to go to the bathroom. He stopped and waited for a moment on his way back to his bedroom to find his parents were still quarrelling with one another. He felt overwhelmingly broken-hearted as if someone stabbed his innocence to its very core; his callow eyes were terrified and needed to cry but he couldn't; and his limbs were trembling with anxiety as how his legs would be able to take another step. He managed to muster what left in his movement and slipped back unnoticed inside the sanctuary of his boyhood bedroom. Since the moment they came back from the trip, the martial relationship between Jonah and Lima began to deteriorate rapidly, submerging noticeably day by day. The home began to divide against itself and an aura of mystery was engulfing it. Everything was dim and bleak, which left an atmosphere as empty as a Halloween jack-o'-lantern's facial expression where all emotions seized to exist. Everyone was crying silently for ceasefire except Lima who was on the edge at all the times—waiting anxiously for some type of resolution with Jonah. Their problems were accumulated night after night behind their closed bedroom; without having the chance to filter their spoiled and foul words like a machine gun full of tainted words firing nonstop at each other. There were a series of questions that remained unanswered then.

One late summer afternoon, while Joseph was standing in front of his bedroom window peering out over the sea, a fifteen-year-old boy stopped en route when he spotted him, and said, "Hi, Joseph."

"Hi, you look good, Mo," said Joseph.

"Certainly, I declare I do."

"You are good, plenty good."

"I want you to hear me out, Joe."

"Tell me about it, then!"

"It's confidential. It's beyond important." Mo said. Something dropped inside Joseph.

"Are you kidding?"

"I wish I was."

Without the slightest hesitation, Joseph vacated the apartment and ran down the stairs like one o'clock. His face was apoplectic with frown and was completely puzzled, when he spotted Mo standing at the entrance of the building. "You have a secret! What secret?"

Mo took a pack of smokes out of his khaki pants side pocket, and a lighter from his white short sleeved shirt pocket. Then he lit the cigarette and took a deep breath while the front cigarette was glowing in the afternoon-sun, and said, "How are you today?"

"All right I guess."

"Listen up, Joe, and listen to me very carefully . . . woman at night comes to your building and spills something onto the main entrance." Mo imparted the secret to Joseph.

"Oh, come off it."

"Like what I've told you."

"I wonder. Go ahead."

"I wonder if you wonder. Like what you know, my own dad doesn't know that I smoke. Every night I sneak out of our apartment and hide behind our building for few drags. Two nights ago just around midnight, I saw a woman sneaking out of our building, don't know which apartment, and heading for your building—"

"Who is that woman?"

"I don't know who she is. She was covering herself completely with a black ragged sheet, leaving only one eye uncovered, like a peephole, which guides her through the way."

"Did you follow her?"

"I tagged her from a distance, I was in fear of being discovered, I am extra careful and extra cautious kind of a guy."

"What was she spilling?"

"Once she arrived at the main entrance door of your building, she brings out a bottle from under her raggedy sheet and then she begins pouring it over the doorway, while she was moving around and around like merry-go-round."

"How many times was she at my place?"

"Last night was the third night in a row that she was in front of your place."

"Have you seen her in the neighborhood during the daytime?"

"Not in the daytime, but in the nighttime, yes, I did see her."

"Maybe, she is some kind of a dope!"

"No way, Jose; she isn't a nincompoop."

"You think so, huh?"

"She is a chock-full of mystery, that old crone."

"Some critters are just bad."

"Some people are just plain bad, you've said . . . yeah . . . hell of a bad. Bad people do bad things. That's where it ends."

Joseph spoke cordially, "Well, thanks Mo, for your private eye show. Your insight on this matter is greatly appreciated." He shook hands with him. "Hey, Mo," he said. "Kindly inform me when this happens again, huh?"

Mo gave him an apprehensive look; then he released his cigarette butt onto the ground and stamped it under his right sneaker. "Leastwise, I'll do my best. Don't fret over it."

"That's a cordial of you, Mo."

"Bye, Joe, for now. I will be watching out for her, I certainly will." Then, he abruptly took a powder.

Joseph returned back home to the solitude of his bedroom, dissected over Mo's words. He doubted whether his story was true, and he was puzzled about what to do next. However, he remained mute about it and kept it to himself.

The next morning, Mo was found dead! The local police found him lying deceased behind the apartment building where he once resided. He was stained with blood covering his eyes, ears, nose, and mouth. Very little was known about the facts behind his mysterious death; there were no witnesses to his sudden demise. The day after his bizarre final exit, Mo was buried in the town cemetery. "Death caused by a massive brain hemorrhage" was written on his death certificate. His death certificate had clearly been falsified, as no one attempted to unravel the mystery surrounding his untimely end. A massive storm of hearsay spread after his tragic fate, some tongues in the neighborhood were wagging that he didn't die from natural causes, he died from unnatural causes—he was murdered. Joseph had an extremely sorrowful time, coming to terms over Mo's quietus. He anxiously buried himself in his tomb of a room to ponder over what Mo had told him about the mystery woman.

The day after Mo was laid to rest; Joseph told his mother about what Mo had informed him about an apparition of a woman who was loitering around the main doorway of their building at night. She looked at him for a moment, and then said, "A life driven by your mind is much better than a life driven by people's words." Then she returned quickly back to her own bedroom.

Lima's tepid marriage and home life faced a new course of challenges, when a mystery woman began to appear at night, but not every night at the main doorway of the building. The marital woes between Lima and her husband, Jonah, began to deteriorate day by day and night after night, until their problems soared sky-high and jetted out of control. They steered into a dark cul-de-sac in their marital roadway and fell prey to a divorce-hunter. Jonah didn't dilly-dally around in divorcing his wife; he divorced her with a colossal amount of rancour and moved out of the martial home to live with his sister, Eve. Finally, the divorce bowed to the unknown power.

From an early age, the youngsters understood the mixture of feelings of missing their father presence and living with their mother. When the marriage veered off the window, Aunt Eve sailed in to take control—the kids had an open door invitation from their aunt to visit their father anytime their hearts and tip-toes desired.

One early afternoon, Joseph decided to pay a visit to his father, alone, without the presence of his brothers. He needed to display his assurance of his unwavering devotion as cordially as possible between himself and his father. That afternoon, after Joseph respectively kissed his Father's hand, he sat next to his father and remained at his side without speaking a single word, at first.

"Joseph, did you know that young man, Mo, who suddenly died last month?" his father said.

"Yes, I knew him, Father."

"Someone saw you with him, maybe a day before he died, standing in front of our building, talking to each other."

"Who was that person?"

"Forshilla."

His name flashed into Joseph's mind, "The rotten-egg head, that Maltese bum, Forshilla!"

"Talk to me, Son?"

"Yes, Father." His voice was parched and barely audible.

His father nodded his head. "Go ahead, then."

"Mo told me about a woman who was hanging around the main doorway of our building at night."

"Did he tell you about where she was residing?

"She was residing at the same building where Mo's family resides."

"Did he tell you anything else?"

"There is nothing more to tell, Father."

"Did you like him?"

"Not in the least."

His father looked up at him, and said, "Crime is here, I hear . . . we have to go to the police at once, and tell them what you've told me, right?"

Joseph nodded in agreement.

"Let's go, then, Son."

"Okay, Father."

The detective listened to Joseph in the diminutive detail. He gathered all the information from him regarding the unknown woman, and let it filter gradually to his file through his pencil. "No tip is too small. The only thing that we're supposed to do is to be vigilant until the end. Vigilant in the little things," said the detective. "I'd like to thank you Joseph very much, for your courage to come here, to the police station; and to tell us about what you heard from Mo Dajaja, before he died. You've done a good deed for the public service. I thank you both for being good citizens. Thank you Mr. Kadprist, and special thanks to the good young man, Joseph."

Within twenty-four hours of Joseph and his father's visit to the police station, a fifty-five-year-old woman and fifty-five-year-old man were arrested in connection with the murder of Mo Dajaja and they were escorted behind bars. Fungista was hefty in built, five feet, six inches tall with short thin brown hair. She had an evil nose of a witch, brown marble eyes with drooping eyelids to match, and horse's mouth filled with yellow crooked teeth. She wore a black ankle length dress and stained white shoes. Fandango was six foot tall, slim, bald, and had a noticeable deep zigzag scar on his cheek underneath his left black eye. There was a touch of evilness around his eyes. He wore white trousers with a ragged white long shirt and a pair of dirty gray sneakers. They both had dark complexions; and shared one entity—illiteracy.

Investigations revealed nothing but shock—she was the same woman that Mo described to Joseph; and she was residing in the same building where Mo had once lived. She confessed only that she felt too sympathetic toward her twin brother, Fandango, when he came from the Derwishieland to visit her, last month; and he was very vengeful toward a woman who threw his headgear onto the incense burner, back at the Derwishieland. She told the police investigator that her brother, Fandango, already knew who she was.

"Who was she?" said the detective.

"Lima," said Fungista.

"How did your brother, Fandango, know where she lives?"

"I told him."

"What is she to you?"

"I don't know her, and she doesn't know me. We never met with each other."

"You had been seen around Lima's place at night. Can you explain what you are doing at the main doorway of her building at night?"

"My brother, Fandango, ordered me to do something for him—"

"Ordered you, huh!"

"Yes, he ordered me."

"Everyone is the master of his own, but not of the others, huh?"

"I was brainwashed into seeing him as a blessed man. I was weak—"

"Keep talking."

"Fandango ordered me to spill some liquid over the main doorway of Lima's building."

"Was it water or oil, or what?"

"I don't know; it was some type of a liquid, that's all I know."

"That was a barrel full of fun to deliver a liquid to Lima's place, huh?"

"My twin brother said, 'It's payback time!'"

"Is that all?"

"That's all, sir."

He stared up at her and spent few moments sizing her up. "Did you murder Mo Dajaja?"

"No, sir," she answered briefly.

"Are you sure you didn't murder him?"

"If I am lying, I am dying."

"Who killed Mo Dajaja, then?"

"I can't tell when I don't know."

Fandango refused to say anything at first; he totally denied the charge. But when the interrogation process took another turn, he cracked like a walnut under the foot whipping and confessed.

"When did you kill Mo Dajaja exactly; give us the exact time?" asked the police interrogator.

"I had no intention at all to kill him. He had some loose screws in his head. I just wanted to fasten them," Fandango babbled.

"Answer the question?"

"Around one o'clock in the morning; but I didn't kill him."

"On what day did you kill Mo Dajaja?"

"I didn't mean to kill him . . . It was an accident. It was Wednesday."

"Where did you find and kill Mo Dajaja?"

"My intent was not to kill him . . . it was behind the building where he lives."

"Tell me how you killed, Mo Dajaja?"

"I didn't kill him; it was an accident. I just used a screwdriver to repair his mind. I just put a screwdriver in his ear to fasten some unfastened screws in his head."

"How did you know his mind was unscrewed?"

"I saw him doing bad deeds, things that are plain wrong."

"Like what?"

"I saw him stalking my sister, Fungista, many times at night."

"Nonsense; whatever the reasons; to kill somebody deliberately is a murder."

"I didn't kill him. I tried to fix his head—"

"What was your motive for murder, of Mo Dajaja?"

"Whatever it was, I didn't do it."

"You have to admit the truth that you killed Mo Dajaja."

"Admit what, you got to be kidding!"

"You gave your sister a liquid to spill it over Lima's place; what was it?"

"It was water mixed with my blessing."

"Do you know Lima?"

"Yes. No."

"What kind of double talk is this?

"Yes, I saw her in the Derwishieland, once; and I don't know her. I saw her as a short-fused woman. I want to help her, that's all."

"You are not a murderer but you are also a sorcerer."

"No, I am not a murderer or a sorcerer. I am a derwish."

"What is your job?"

"A derwish—"

"A man with the mind of a derwish, faces a dim future in the real world. You went too far this time, Derwish. You will be on trial for the murder of Mo Dajaja."

Fandango Calanka pleaded innocent to the murder charge. The jury found him guilty of the crime with which he was charged—they reached a unanimous verdict of "guilty of first-degree murder" in death of Mo Dajaja. Fandango pleaded to the judge, begging him for leniency. The Judge said: "I have to proclaim this before I pronounce your sentence, 'Your egregious crime is an abomination to all mankind. You brought disgrace onto yourself by this nefarious crime. You are a demon masquerading as a human being. You are an evil man!" Then he sentenced him to his death, by hanging.

Fungista Calanka pleaded ignorance of any wrongdoing, during her trial. The jurors found her guilty of felony convictions, for harboring the killer, Fandango Calanka, and the illegal practice of sorcery. She was sentenced four to ten years in prison (she could be released as early as four years if she serves her sentence with good behavior, but if she causes any sort of trouble while in prison, she could be held as long as ten years).

One day Jonah said to Joseph, "Joseph, you like to write stories."

And Joseph said, "Yes, I do."

Then Jonah said, "Someday when you are ready, you might write our family stories. Only then you will understand what happened and why?"

"Yes, Father."

Jonah spoke wisely, "Keep the doorway of the past tilted, never take your head out of the memory-sand; and swing the doorway of the future wide open." His eyes of life glittered with hope. "Oh, Joseph," he said. "I am quite certain that one day our memories will be cuddling your imaginary horizon. After all, life is an acquisition of memories, and that's all there is left."

Later in life when an invisible thread connected Joseph with a collection of memories from his past, he wrote the "Doorways" in a style regardless of time, place and circumstances; as his father always said, "Physical objects can vanish without trace, but not memories. An invisible thread connects us with the memories, regardless of time, place and circumstances; the thread may stretch or tangle; but it will never break."

That was the landmark memories of the trip to the Derwishieland; and that was a story of several stories and plots . . . a living puzzle of life itself.

Doorway Two

The Missing Time

The House of Al

It was on that particular summer afternoon, the sun was shining brightly; and the overall ambience of the apartment was brimming overly with warmth. Lima spotted her son standing at the frame of the kitchen door. "What are you up to?"

"Would you please let me go to my uncle's home; feel like staying overnight, please, Mom?" the ten-year-old Joseph said. "I did my homework. I was a good boy, wasn't I?" He waited anxiously for her response!

"You are as shifty as smoke, but I don't mind if you visit your uncle."

"Is it okay with you, Mother, if I stay overnight?"

She spoke in a pleasant tone, "You come back here tomorrow morning, nine o'clock sharp." She raised her well groomed eyebrows. "Nine o'clock sharp in the morning," she said. "Go on then, enjoy yourself, you have earned it." The green light was given to Joseph to visit and stay overnight at his uncle's home.

His appreciation technique kicked in. "You made me plum happy," he said, "thank you, Mother."

"Nine o'clock in the morning."

He responded happily, "Nine of the clock, on the level." He made his move into his room. "Thanks, Man Above," he whispered. "The good time is just in site."

His thirty-three-year-old mother was five feet, two inches; slim, with black short hairstyle. She dressed herself in different types of brightly colored dresses, with colorful silk scarves. She had neither weak nerve nor fearful bone in her petite frame; and had the gift to radiate powerful abilities, that even certain animal species could sense it, and that was her forte. She portrayed herself as a direct to the point kind of a woman, with no beating around the bush type; and she had absolute zero tolerance for the numskulls of the world.

He was granted the green light to visit his uncle, which lit up his heart with childhood joyfulness. He dashed through the dining room to his bedroom; opening his bedroom dresser drawers and selected his attire for the special occasion; grey shorts, white T-shirt and socks. He picked up his black shoes by the main door, put them on, and said, "Thank you, Mother, for letting me visit my uncle."

"Remember, I got a sky full of angels watching over you."

"By golly, is that true?"

"Yes, it is true. They see you, but you can't see them."

"How about you, Mother, can you see them?"

"Yes, I can see them."

"What do they look like?"

"They look like Egrets."

"They are large white birds, aren't they?"

"They are indeed."

"Do you talk to them, angels?"

"They only whisper in my ears and tell me everything about you and your brothers."

"Oh, oh, oh, oh, Mother. Tell me more, Mother?"

"Not everything you know eases your curiosity. Some things in life are more beautiful if they remain unsaid."

"Hmm—"

"Get going Son! Say, hi to your uncle and your Aunt Maryouma, will you?"

"Will do, Mother—"

"And don't forget to come back tomorrow morning at nine."

"I'll be back tomorrow morning at nine."

"That's to be expected."

"Good-bye, Mother." He walked quickly out of the apartment, hopping and skipping from a single step to another as he went down along the meandering staircase. He was born and raised with his other three brothers in a four-room apartment. The three-story building had only three apartments; his family occupied the second floor; while the ground and third floors were occupied by two Italian families—namely, Morelli and Chechinto.

He rushed from the building and walked quickly along the neighborhood street; he then slowed down and paused in front of a Catholic Church. There was an overly tall mahogany type hard brown wooden door at the entrance of the church, lined at the sides with two small-sized brown wooden doors. He walked curiously up the church steps, and stood in front of the main massive brown door entrance. His youthful curious mind filled with an inquisitive question, *"What lies behind this tall frosty brown door?"* He cautiously pushed open the massive door, and the first thing emerged from behind the door was a thunderous sounds of a church organ. He viewed with wondering eyes, he was surprised by what he saw—few parishioners were sitting on seemed to be uncomfortable wooden pews, they were like a silent choir in a captured hypnotic glaze, fixated upon a golden elaborate crucifix, which was in full display behind the altar. The curious visitor, Joseph, also discovered statues of saints mounted on the cold inner walls of the church, between the brightly stained-glass windows. There were lit candles and oil scents which filled the church with light and comforting aromas while consuming their tranquil scenery. He pondered for few moments before his fear geared up a few notches; his innocent eyes caught a nun dressed head to toe in black—full nun's habit—was staring straight at him; he then decided at once to vacate the unfamiliar scene immediately.

After he left the house of prayer, he went on walking, heading toward his elementary school. He paused for a while and gazed into the window of his classroom. He had a sudden flashback memory of what transpired the day before in his math class—dialogues between his math teacher and a student, and his everlasting stimulus of words to study with a sense of vigor:

"Three multiply by three?" the math teacher, Fleshy Nose, said. He pointed his arrow like finger at one of his students, Bow Legs, and barked at him to answer.

"Nine," Bow Legs answered skittishly.

"Stand up and on the double to the blackboard, and write, 'Three multiply by three equals nine.'"

Trembling with trepidation, Bow Legs quivery rose up and hesitantly proceeded forward to the blackboard. The teacher handed him the chalk and demanded him to write the answer. He grabbed the chalk with trembling fingers and wrote "3x3=" then he stopped.

"Write the answer?" Fleshy Nose barked out.

Bow Legs drew a loop and began looping continuously over the loop like a speeding car which lost its brakes around roundabout; and then drew a horizontal line.

"Make a loop and then draw a line like an arrow looking down, that's the way to make a nine."

The apprehensive, Bow Legs, tried in vain to bring the nine's tail down, but he couldn't; he couldn't draw a vertical line of the number nine! The math teacher reacted swiftly and asked Bow Legs to go back to his seat.

When the math teacher heard some students were giggling behind their stubby hands; he surveyed the students and spent few moments gazing over those whom caught his attention, and said, "It might seem amusing, if you all will become doctors, engineers, lawyers, teachers, et cetera, et cetera; then who will sweep the streets, polish shoes, collect the rubbish from the streets, and who will do the laundry, et cetera, et cetera. Some of you will be doctors, or bootblacks. Some of you will be engineers, or street cleaners. Some of you will be lawyers, or trash-collectors. Some of you will be teachers, or work down the hall peeling potatoes for lunch in the kitchen of this school . . ."

The students looked at their math teacher with bated breath.

The math teacher continued, "It's what it is."

"It's what it is," Joseph said. He repeated what the teacher had said word for word.

The journey to his uncle's home continued after a long pause in front of his school. He went on walking along a narrow street, until he reached a peculiar place where everyone tried to avoid it like the Black Death—a wooden rickety shack with a tin roof between two high buildings—known as the shack of evil. The oddball character who resided in the shack was well known to everyone in the neighborhood, his name was Farro, and he was living all alone in the shack except with his loyal companion, the moonshine still. He was the only one running a still back in those days. He was six feet tall, thirty-year-old colossal black man; he had a rounded pumpkin face with wide white circles as pealed boiled eggs around his black eyes, and a massive burly Fort Knox of a forehead, as it was coated with cast iron—that was his signature forte. He had no mention of any kin, and nobody could answer the jigsaw puzzle of his birthplace. Nearly everyone in the town tried to avoid all physical contact with him and his publicized forehead knockouts—where they saw him, they ran racing the wind. *"Keep away from that black evil; he is wicked as it comes . . . here's what you do if you see him across the street . . . keep a distance and leave your legs racing with the pace of the wind . . . disappear on the double,"* that was the hush-hush piece of advice from every parent to their youngsters. Joseph wasn't apprehensive about Farro, as his father didn't ever mention his name to anyone. He glanced at the condemned shack, curious to catch a quick glimpse of Farro and then he turned away—there was no clear sign of the neighborhood outcast at his own seedy hideout of a shack.

He then continued walking on a narrow soil road toward his uncle's house; there were few residential houses smelled of dust and age on both sides along the road. His uncle's one-story house stood alone at the end of the road with its whitish walls, poorly maintained two bay windows, and an aged green front door, as if it were worn out from the numerous knocks on it during its long days.

He knocked at the main door of his uncle's house once, twice, thrice; and waited at the door. A sweet soft voice subsequently penetrated from the door. "Who is there?"

He became relaxed at her voice. "It's me . . . Joseph."

She opened the door, and smiled warmly at him. "Come on in, Joseph; come on in; how are you?"

"I'm fine."

"How's your mother?"

"She is fine."

"Come on in, then."

Maryouma was a twenty-five-year-old woman, medium height on the slim side—and was always tastefully dressed—she had brownish eyes, medium length jet-black-hair. Her fresh-faced voice was as soft as a kitten, and had warm-sweet demure as if it was gifted from heaven above.

He followed her, down the tiled stairs, to a large roofless hall. The home comprised of one bedroom, a combined living and dining room, bathroom, and a kitchen. She took the lead to the living room-dining room combination while he was happily ambling behind her. She announced him to her husband and then left the room.

"Hi Joseph, how are you?" Uncle Al said. He relaxed in a chair sipping his afternoon tea, while he was smoking his favorite brand of cigarette.

"Hi Uncle, I am good," said Joseph.

Al was thirty years of age, five feet four inches tall, with short styled black hair, and deep brown eyes. He was a habitual smoker, he always had a cigarette nearby while having his tea or coffee, after meals.

Joseph went and sat beside his uncle. He had a puzzled look toward his uncle, and said, "Why is everyone in this town scared of Farro?"

"He's an oddball type of a character," Al said. "Let me tell you a story: Once upon a time there lived a lion that roamed the prairie. One day while it was sleeping, a silly and mindless mouse jumped on his frontal paws. The lion became overly impatient while it was witnessing the disrespectful behavior of the mouse. The lion was way beyond furious at the mouse; then it decided to teach the pest of the mouse a useful life lesson. The lion caught the annoyed mouse between its front paws, glared absolutely repulsive at it, and said, 'You make a sport of me, huh! I'd rather starve to death than chew on a shrimp of a mouse like you.' The mouse begged for his short tale of a life and said to the lion, if you set me free, one day I will return the favor to you. The lion sarcastically roared with laughter and then paw punched the mouse between its beady-eyed face . . . one day not long after that, the lion was caught in a hunter's net, unable to free himself. The lion filled the plains with its angry outreaching roars. The mouse knew that the lion was in a big time trouble . . . the mouse bravely approached the lion and tore the snare by its razor sharp teeth and sets the lion free. After that incident, the lion befriended the mouse, but the mouse remained overly cautious and prepared for a possible escape hatch of a plan from the lion." He took a sip of his tea, and added, "Like some people . . . some people behave like lions, and some people behave like mice."

"It's a mighty good story! Is old Farro a lion or mouse, then?"

"Some people in our fair city find Farro is very useful like the mouse in the story . . . some people ask for his help when they fall prey to an aggressor. Any problem shared with Farro is a problem solved; he has one sure effective method of tackling any problem . . . he sizes up the situation very quickly, and when push comes to shove, he always uses his forehead; he swings his forehead with all his strength and KO 'knockout' the aggressor on the face. His powerful forehead is the only tool he needs to make a fast buck. His nickname is Hammer Head, and that is that; old school method but it is still effective."

"It's forbidden by law."

"Absolutely—"

"And customs, too."

"That as well; be careful, Joseph."

"Be careful of what?"

"Everything . . . just keep your nose clean."

"I shall, Uncle."

Joseph looked quickly away, for what he had learned about Farro. He left the room; then he went to the kitchen where he sensed the presence of Maryouma. The kitchen was located in the right-side wall from the combined living and dining room area. The air of the kitchen smelled of fresh fried fish, and the sizzling and spattering of hot oil in the open pan generated such a heat that other items in the kitchen could ignite off-hand. The floor of the kitchen was roughly seventy square feet, and had smoky vinyl sheet flooring. The kitchen had a brown wooden cabinet with single doors, filled with an assortment of dishes and cutleries; below the cabinet, laid a white tiled counter, and a stainless-steel sink. A white four-burner gas stove was located next to the kitchen counter, and a newly white refrigerator was located further away from the stove. Everything in the kitchen was in immaculate order, and in good taste.

"How are you, Joseph?" Maryouma said. She began to merrily moving about the kitchen, while she was preparing the evening meal.

"Fine Auntie," Joseph said.

"I hope you are not too fussy about my evening menu."

"I always enjoy your food; in fact, I can eat anything from your hands with pleasure."

She raised her well-shaped eyebrows and lowered her soft voice, "I want to have a young man just like you, thoughtful, clever and well mannered."

"Thank you, Aunt Maryouma."

She nodded in agreement. "Yes, you are."

She gathered up the delicious dishes of delectable cuisines on to a large rounded silver tray from the kitchen and lovingly carried them into the combined living and dining room. One section of the combined rooms was arranged as a living room, and the other section was arranged as a dining room. The living room had one brown sofa that lay against one of the four cloudy peach walls; a dark walnut end table was by the second wall; a vintage gazelle velvet tapestry was hanging on the third wall; and an alternating ticking sound of a German cuckoo clock was displayed in the middle of the fourth wall. In the center of the living room lay a scatter red rug and on top of it was a small dark walnut table with four matching chairs. A large vintage burgundy rug was laid in the other section, surrounded by an assortment of firm settee cushions covered by tawny-orange fabrics, and some thick wall pads with yellow fabrics against the three-cornered walls. Both rooms had circular white pendant lamps. Even though the scents of tobacco and the heat which was filtering around the combined rooms were not conductive to a hearty appetite, the two combined rooms resembled each other in taste.

The platter of lemony fried mackerel with seasoned rice was placed in the middle on a mat of the large rug. They sat around the ample platter, and between the three of them they feasted on everything that was before them. After nightly feast, they had sweet bite-size apple dumplings for dessert, while Al was flipping on the radio to listen to the 7:00 p.m. news.

Joseph turned to his uncle, "Do you know him, Uncle?"

"Who is him?" Al said.

"Farro."

"He is a piece of work . . . I pay him no mind."

"Farro is very useful to fools like him," Maryouma said. Then she went off without making a slightest of sound into the hallway with the tray of empty dishes, straight to the kitchen.

"A fool always finds a bigger fool to admire him. It's what it is," said Al.

"Did you ever meet him at all, Uncle?" said Joseph.

"Two days ago I saw him loitering around in the market; rummaging around with his wide bullfrog eyes and bullying in the market while he was doing his own shoplifting wide open. Most traders in the market were avoiding him like the bubonic plague; and fear him for not paying the value of what he was not buying—he takes whatever he wants, whenever he wants, without paying a single cent—I pay him no respect, I pay him no regard. I pay him no mind."

"Is Farro his real name, then?"

"No. Farro perceived as characteristically 'ferrum' a Latin word for iron."

"So that is his nickname?"

"Yes, and his nickname made him hard-headed."

"Do you know his real name?"

"Yes. His real name is Bosadia It."

"Does he have a family?"

"He has no family to speak of. No one knew from where he came from, he has no friends, too . . . no one desires his friendship except for those who uses him for their own illegal services." Then, changing the subject, he added, "Forget him, he is a skank, he is a piece of nothing. Don't mention him, he's quite a bum. What do you want to be when you grow up?"

"I want to be a scientist."

"Tomorrow belongs to those who study and prepare for today."

"Sure."

"Where the education is shallow, no country will sail. Education is the passport to a prosperous future."

"Indeed."

"The first element of success is to succeed at home. Success in life is nothing more than two schools to follow, your mother and school."

"Father, too."

"Listen to them, and learn from them . . . your mother and father and your school."

Maryouma opened the door and peeped in. "Time for bed. It's nine o'clock," she said. She left quietly.

Joseph and his uncle both slept on twin mattresses on the living room floor.

"Good night, Uncle."

"Good night, Joseph."

The light went off as Joseph tried sensibly to be as soundless as the night-ward sky in his movement and breath. The living room was filled with the aroma of his uncle's cigarette smoke curled in the air, mixed with the lingering exotic scent of his aunt's distinctive perfume. He was overwhelmed with the hospitality of the day from both his aunt and uncle. His unconscious mood poured over his mind as his sleepy head touched the pillow and that moment he realized right away that there was something missing, his own bed's pillow at his family's home. Despite the difference in the bed accommodations, he fell fast asleep with a full belly and a gleeful heart.

He woke up around midnight scratching frantically at a constant itching sensation all over his body. He felt as his whole body was being eaten alive by mosquitos! The uncomfortable sensation of the persistent itching made him leave the combined living and dining room at once. He quietly closed the door behind him and a figure came into his peripheral vision; he found himself standing face to face with an image of a woman in a shape of a mammoth blazing fireball, staring down at him with her sinister bloodshot eyes. She was perched up on the edge of the roof, between the bathroom and Maryouma's bedroom, glaring down at him. The bitterly cold breeze caused his bare feet to freeze while a foul stench of rotten meat, covered with filthy-flies, was invading in the roofless hallway. The apparition like was ten feet wide by ten feet in height, shining with a dazzling red and yellow light, except for her/its bloodshot unlatching dead set eyes. She/it was a flickering flame figure with a silent like unbridled keenness. He stood in dread for a few unconscionable moments, breathing shakily between his cold unsteady hands—he was stark raving mad as a hatter.

What Joseph came across that indelible night was just a fourteen-karat coincidence. What a coincidence that he was in that hall at the same time as the apparition! It wasn't a nickel and dime kind of a show. It was a real show! It was evident that he was under the influence of an apparition. The apparition obscured his vision and hindered his breathing. Subsequently, his mind was occupied with an assortment surreal of images. He was in grave danger, but his fear over-shadowed the danger. The floor boards felt uneven under his bare feet. He couldn't recollect where he was or how he arrived there. What he witnessed that momentous night became ever so clear and matching the modus operandi of an apparition. He turned his head slightly, and looked up the apparition; then, he raised his trembling right hand upward like a blindfold to cover his innocent eyes and turned back toward the wall of the combined living and dining room. His first knee-jerk reaction was to run back to his safe haven bed, but he felt that his legs were bound with canine chain—he couldn't move an inch from his designated place. He began to shiver in a state of frigid fear as he felt the apparition was staring through him with her/its demon like transfixed eyes—he became a prisoner, locked and monitored by a combination of fear and danger. Unconsciously, by force of both fear and danger, his tongue was held hostage in his desert-dry mouth while his motionless body was trembling as a hunted prey in an irreversible trap. He was so terrified his legs were wobbling, and his body became entirely unrelated to his mind—he lost the complete control of himself.

He screamed at the top of his youthful lungs, "Help me, Uncle; help me, Aunt. Help, help, help…" His voice trailed off into far off silence. He felt an urgent urge to reach out for his uncle and aunt. He repeatedly shrieked out for help, his voice was inaudible to the human ear but was only audible to the awaiting apparition. The distinctive stench of decayed meat lingered in the hall. He found himself as a microorganism under the microscopic supervision of a wraith—as a lightening spot as the moon for the ghost. He clung to the moon lit wall for some sort of barrier and felt as an icy knife was playing demented game of tic-tac-toe on his shivering spine. That one unimaginable night turned out to be one way detour into cul-de-sac of a living hell! The apparition began listening to his shriek while he was shrieking like one who awakens from the grave; and peering at him while he was shivering as Oliver Twist begging for a second helping of cold porridge. The phantom kept her/its eyes wide open at him, just like a bald eagle about to swoop in with ease on its spotted prey.

Trembling with terror, he opened his quivery-mouth with a trembling whisper, "Where is she?"

He waited for a few lasting seconds; then, strangely enough, he turned and had a quick browse around, seeking out the apparition. A likeness of a woman in a shape of a titanic-size blazing fireball; clearly became visible to him as she/it was peering upon him from the edge of the tiled roof. He felt the sway of the floor under his feet, and began to sway from side to side/backward and forward, realizing that his uncle's home was haunted by some type of a ghastly-ghostly image. There was a demonic haunting expression in the apparition's red filled departed eyes. He was haunted by the fear that he was an unchallenging prey for the ghost, ready to be stalked and slayed. Then he felt that somebody touched and rotated him, one hundred eighty degrees; he found himself facing the wall, once again. He found himself held hostage by the ghost; and his horror began to overtake him! And suddenly he found himself at the bedroom door of his aunt. He tried in vain to open her bedroom door, but discovered it to be locked. He ran to where his uncle slept, he tried in vain to open the door, but he found it to be locked, also. He had an overpowering sense that the ghost was the suspect whom locked both doors in a mysterious-calculated plan. He had no other choice, as his young life was in a grave state of danger; he extemporaneously ran to the kitchen, opened the door, rushed inside, and bolted the kitchen door from inside. He stood firmly against the secured kitchen door, thinking he was going to hell in a handcart—he was incommunicado, in the kitchen.

The naked light bulb dangled from the kitchen ceiling suddenly began to flicker; then the flickering ceased on to the 'light' mode. The kitchen was dark as a yawning grave—he was horrified and mystified by his perilous situation. He was very unsteady on his feet while he was groping for the light switch; he switched the light on; then without hesitation switch it off. He returned back to his chosen safe place and stood behind the bolted door in the darken kitchen; then, he decided to move to the left side of the locked door, anticipating the presence of the ghost in any moment. He was engulfed with terror as he was eavesdropping behind the barrier of the bolted kitchen door on the approaching spirit. Within a second or so he began to observe something strange—a fainted light haloed underneath the kitchen door.

"Please, leave me alone, please!" he whispered.

Something caught his attention—the limited peephole let in some light—he turned his head and squinted through the peephole. He peeped through the peephole into the hall, to discover the whole hall was glowing with the light. A tidal wave of horror rolled his way when he glimpsed, a ghost-like woman was descending silently to the hall. Like a canary in a coal mine, the light began to sweep through the floor underneath the kitchen door. The blinding light stood luminously inside the kitchen, causing his eyes and mind to shut down; then, he vanished. He was kidnaped, not killed. There was no two ways about it; he was abducted from the kitchen and from his uncle's home. His unconscious journey to the unknown world lasted approximately eight hours.

Nine o'clock in the morning, the kitchen door flung opened. Maryouma muttered nervously, "Here you are!" Her voice began to quaver. "Oh, Joseph," she said. "Where have you been? Your uncle and I were searching for you everywhere all night and all morning! Where have you been hiding?"

Joseph paused with anxiety, and his mind was racing against time! "What time is it now?" he said.

"It's nine o'clock. It's Friday morning; where have you been?"

"I was in the kitchen—"

"No, you weren't in the kitchen, and you weren't anywhere in the house. Did you go home, or what? Tell me the truth, where have you been hiding all night and part of the morning?"

"I left the bedroom area and found a scary ghost sitting on the edge of the roof, glaring down upon me. I wanted to go back to the bedroom, but it was closed off. I tried to harbor in your room, but found the door also locked. I ran away from the ghost and harbored in the kitchen. Only ten minutes ago—"

"There is no ghost in this house, and elsewhere."

"Yes, there is a ghost in this house."

"Hold your horses, Joseph; there is no ghost in my home."

"I saw it."

"You've seen nothing; it's all in your imagination."

"There is nothing more to tell, Aunt Maryouma." He left her and never set foot in his uncle's home ever again.

There was a horrendous opponent working against his story—

who was ready to believe what he witnessed that night in his uncle's home. Would his mother or father hear him out, and believe him? He returned home and was hoping against hope that there might be something in there that would reassure him into what he saw in his uncle's place.

His mother was waiting outside the main door as he emerged. "Good morning, Joseph," she said. "How's your mini vacation to your uncle's home?"

Joseph muttered nervously, "Good morning, Mother." He was shaking like a dice-box. "Oh, Mother," he said. "I will never visit his place, again."

"Golly Joseph, why's that?"

"I saw a ghost in his place."

"You saw what!"

"I saw a ghost inside his house, Mother."

"I wonder!"

"I saw a woman in a shape of a fire-ball with big red eyes." He told his mother what occurred the night before.

His mother slowly turned her head and looked at him, and said, "You had a psychic dream, Joseph. Don't breathe a single word to anyone; not a single word. If you tell people something like this, they will start gossiping. And consequently, you lose your self-respect. In life you can lose anything except your respect."

He listened to several of his mother's quotations, but "in life you can lose anything except your self-respect" was his lifelong favorite.

An hour in the afternoon before lunch, his fifty-six-year-old father knocked and entered his bedroom, and said, "Look Joseph, The oldest and strongest emotion of mankind is fear, and the oldest and strongest kind of fear is fear of the unknown." He patted Joseph on the shoulder and left the bedroom.

That was the most nightmarish experience Joseph had ever suffered; and it was the worst night of his entire life. He remembered the circumstances of that fateful night and tried to abreact it, but the inescapable memories had a lifelong effective powerful hold to torment him. The magnitude of the horror at the sight of that night remained an enigmatic mystery which lingered silently in his haunted memory throughout his entire life.

Since that night of mystery, his ray of thoughts orbited many countless times around the earth, hoping to solve the mystery about the secret of that haunted night. What a secret that remains! It remained an ambiguous night and was not fully resolved—no answer to what happened that night to Joseph at his uncle's home. That was a mysterious night, and what a secretive night it was in Joseph's life. Since that night his life began to transform, especially at night when he was all alone in a completely secluded and secure refuge in his bedroom. He began to hear fainted beep-like sounds; at the beginning his attention wasn't distracted, but one night he decided to focus on the whistling sound. Whenever he heard the sound, it became clear night after night, until he reached a level where he began to hear whispering sound within that whistling sound. One night he focused on the whispering voices, and discovered that they are voices that spoke about his past, present and even what will transpire in his future. He realized that he must be vigilant to those sounds, which did not come out of the blue, they came from something-somewhere, and that thing wouldn't accept those who eavesdrop on their whispering. One night he decided not to listen for the start of sounds, hoping against hope that the doppelganger did not track him down back to his home. He continued to ignore hearing the ghost whispering for several nights and several weeks. The ghost whispers began to diminish little by little from night after night and when the ghost realized that Joseph wasn't curious enough about its whisperer; the whispers eventually faded away; and one night the ghost whispering ceased completely. Since that spine-chilling night, Joseph believed that he had been visited by something/someone; it wasn't a ghost, it was a real woman that appeared from the sky. The story wasn't a spurious story, it was a real one. The memory never failed him; on the contrary, it lasted throughout all of Joseph's life, until he wrote with a short simplicity of style, "The Missing Time."

Doorway Three

Whispers of the Imagination

Pojangles

"This is what we buried together," Sledge said to his twin brother, Sludge.

There were two identical twin brothers, eighteen-year-olds Sledge and Sludge Shishbani; they were five feet tall with medium weights, and appeared unshaven and ill-dressed. They lived in a shack with a dirt floor, and enjoyed the solitude of their own shack life. The desert adopted them since they were orphaned at age of five. They didn't know their origin and the local villagers didn't know either. A donkey had been their constant companion those past years, and it was a faithful companion.

The twenty-five-year-old donkey was unusual donkey. It was five feet tall with a beefy figure. Its coat was soft yellow as liquid honey, and thin as the shadow of a single hair. Its yellow fur flopped over its temple and over its green-apple eyes. Its eyes glowed unnaturally with wisdom. Its head had two ears not like a donkey's ears, but like rosy seashells; and had features of red-nose of a wintry reindeer, with a mouthpiece of a wise man. It had four legs similar to human legs with four emerald hooves, similar to its soulful eyes; and had a multi-color kite of a tail. It shook its head up and down for yes; and right and left for no; and seemed to whisper with wisdom. It sat like a human, with its legs crossed; and slept like a human on its both sides snuggling between Sledge and Sludge. The donkey was not fussy about its food—it survived for long periods only with dates and water.

Sledge and Sludge were very respectful and obedient to their donkey. The donkey carried heavy loads on its back from one village to another; and it was their only source of income and inspiration. The Shishbani Brothers loved the donkey with beloved affection, they adored it, and from their great love for the donkey they kept his branded name as Pojangles, and Pojangles he was. One day while they were transporting goods on his back as they were on their way to a neighboring village in the desert, Pojangles collapsed suddenly on the sand and died instantly. The two brothers buried their beloved donkey, and from their endless love and affection for Pojangles, the Shishbanis buried their four-legged-friend in a final resting place, similar to the grave of a man. The two mourning brothers were beyond despondent for the loss of the four-legged loyal companion, Pojangles. They faithfully grieved next to his grave shedding streams of tears for many scorching days and shivering nights trying to comprehend their untimely loss.

One morning a group of villagers passed by the two brothers and asked them, "Why are you sitting here? Why are you both shedding so many tears?"

The two brothers' tears raced down their grief-stricken cheeks while they were sobbing. "The bond and the aid died, for we had goodness and blessings, and we used him to satisfy our needs, lift our weights, and connect our distances, he died, Pojangles," they said.

The people thought that the two grieving brothers were referring to a holy man or an authority of some guardian from above. The news of Pojangles sudden demise spilled over as a shockwave to them all, and marched out like a procession passed along the street. Some simple-minded people would happily donate their hard-earned money to Sledge and Sludge to the memory of Pojangles. The holy Pojangles' blessings couldn't pour on them without coughing up the dough to either Sledge or Sludge. They paid money just to approach the gravesite of the departed Pojangles, who held the blessings and the dignities. The twin opportunistic brothers, Sledge and Sludge, marveled at the unexpected magical golden goose to lay down cold, hard cash. But after they had been pondering about it for some time; the Shishbanis realized right away that a golden gold mine of opportunity had fallen straight into their greedy twin-laps. At first, the twin brothers built a tent, resembled a miniature circus style tent, on Pojangles' gravesite; then after a brief period of time they built a more sizable-enhancing shrine. Months had passed and people began to chatter about the blessings and dignities of this elder holy man, Pojangles. From the point of view of those naïve people, they believed that Pojangles held the mystical powers of healings the bedridden patients, marrying off the spinsters-prunes, loosening the magic, and solving the unsolvable problems. The twin brothers schemed a boatload of fast cold, hard cash.

One day the two brothers became overly greedy by the other's loot, and the two disagreed over the split of what was considered the flowing gravy train. Sledge demanded more payoffs from their dishonest cash harvest scheme. It teed Sludge off when his brother Sledge demanded more loot from their racketeering charges—Sludge's anger began to surface.

One dark ominous autumn evening, Sludge was absolutely incensed, he yelled, "By Pojangles, I will tell him that you're slicing in to my hard-earned share, give me my cabbage back or I will ask him to take vengeance on you." Then he pointed his forefinger to where Pojangles was buried.

"How dare you speak to me like this?" Sledge said.

"How dare I?"

Sledge laughed like an untangled-escaping loon, "Which holy man are you yapping about?" His voice muttered nervously. "You asshole," he said. "Stop bojangling and realize that it was just an ass! And we buried it together, remember, brother?"

It was a tornado of a shockwave, the first time Sludge heard his brother swear at him. He buried his face in his hands as he was beginning to look the worse for wear, then collapsed at his brother's feet and passed away. Sludge passed on of a broken heart at age of thirty.

Sledge muttered confusingly, "His time was up! There is nothing that can be done now; done and dusted . . . we were best of brothers and friends, and we had big time dreams. We believed in each other. Anyone says otherwise? Well, bless their hearts." He buried his bother next to the grave of Pojangles.

A cloudburst of fortunes had showered heavily upon Sledge after his twin brother, Sludge's abrupt demise. He lived comfortably without lifting a finger.

One day, when Sledge was nearly seventy years old, he met an ambitious young woman with a shady past named Shipoopi Moonercan at Pojangles' shrine and finished up getting hitched to her. He got it wrong from the start as he wasn't aware of the upcoming whirlwind of danger, and that led to a murder.

Shipoopi Moonercan was thirty-two-year-old, five foot five, on the corpulent side with oversized-extending hips and a noticeable caboose. She had black marble eyes, shoulder length wavy brown-hair, and a bit of a snout nose. Her advertising dress style was mainly skin-tight of low-cut short-sleeve shabby floral dresses; and low heel white sandals with open peep toe. She upgraded her image with large sparkly hoop earrings, and with a blue beaded bracelet. Her focal point on her round face was her luscious lips, and her focal point on her chest was a pair of triple D set of headlights.

She claimed Spud and Spade were their offspring, but her claim was an opaque to him. Shipoopi was not the type of a woman to be faithful to any man. She wasn't exactly enamored with the idea of spending her whole life with Sledge—she married him solely for his lucrative gravy train rather than a loyal spin on the marriage-merry-go-round.

One unprecedented night as Sledge woke up from a silent sleep, he heard a hissing sound. Shockingly, he stood up in the dark in a state of fearful-shock and was held hostage by his own tongue. He tended to avoid all physical contact with the hissing sounds and tried to escape, but there was no escape, as his legs became emerged in quicksand. He recoiled in horror, from what he felt as a cold gust of a wintery wind blowing strongly inside his fragile bones. Immediately, he found himself in front of his spouse, Shipoopi, with living snakes in place of hair; and her tongue was as black as a tongue of a queen cobra. Her black tongue was certainly lively and ready for the kiss of death before biting. Her lower frame had turned into a queen cobra with a rattling sound; and the crown of swirling snakes covered her head, were hissing as they were ready to strike their prized prey. He glimpsed at her black marble eyes, tried to avoid her intimidating glare, but he couldn't as he was dead. She looked at him with horrifying eyes, while he was watching her and focusing into her demonic black eyes. Then he paused momentarily with a loud stone click and turned to stone. He was eighty years of age when he died; and she was forty-two years of age at that time. The stone statue displayed Sledge in full stature with full features of his face and body—it was the three-dimensional shape of Sledge Shishbani.

Spud and Spade were both seven-year-olds when Sledge transformed to a stone. They were lanky boys with ponytail bald heads. Some people called them twin Coffee Cakes, because their faces looked like a coffee cake, crunchy texture; and some people referred to them as sp. sp.; but most people called them the Shishbanis. It was tough, not easy, to look at them. Their clothes tended to be similar across entire village. It consists of loose-fitting white long-sleeved shirts, long trousers, and white bob caps for when they were outdoors, to protect them from the sun's rays and to keep them cool. The boys went around barefoot most of the time.

No one knew the real story of Pojangles except Sledge and his deceased brother Sludge. They kept the dark side of Pojangles' secret locked away between them, until the last day of their lives; their secret passed away with them.

The stone statue of Sledge was placed in front of the entrance to Pojangles' tomb and his brother's gravesite. One day, a seventy-year-old partially sighted man named Amia Zomia—he was five feet three inches tall; his skin was brown as leather; he wore a long sleeve white shirt, white trousers, white bobble hat, and was barefooted—came to visit the site of Pojangle's. Amia Zomia was a man who had the unique power to hear sounds and to receive vocal messages from the spirit world, as the voices from the dead. He had the superlative power to hear the dead; he was a clairaudient. He stood in front of the statue of Sledge and began to approach it gradually; then, he put his ear as a stethoscope on the stone statue as he was receiving pulses from it. (Time and chance unveiled all secrets.) He stood stunned while listening to how Sledge departed from this world, how he transformed to a stone while we was alive by his snake of a wife, Shipoopi.

After Sledge was transformed into a stone statue, Shipoopi married five times, in her seventeen years span of time. She could feel the shimmy in the steering wheel of her victim of a spouse; she was attracted only to money like an iron bar to a magnet. It was the money that attracted her to marry the following aging low-level stooges: Big Ben, Bongo along with his twin brother Bingo, Bubbles, and Bolero. She was selecting Bs for husbands, because she was a 'B' herself. She lived in polyandry, two for one deal—she took on Bongo and Bingo as husbands at the same time. Like sunlight, sunset, a husband appeared, a husband disappeared. After a husband got a vigorous sponge all over his deep lining-pockets, he was awarded a good football punt in his rear, and out of her life. The bloodsucking serpent Shipoopi believed that a stooge with unlimited loose change was like a bird with wings; and a stooge with limited loose change was like a bird without wings. It was all about their money to her!

Amia Zomia was a clairaudient; Hortense, was a clairvoyant. They were husband and wife, soul-mates, seekers for mysteries, believed in one another, and they both were diligent detectives for the dead. They lived all their lives in a black goat-hair tent, divided by cloth curtains into rug-floor areas for a sitting room and bedroom.

Hortense was eighty years of age, five feet ten, and her skin was as bronze as her age. Her general outfit was mainly brightly colored blouse with baggy sleeves that were embroidered with beads and baggy silk trousers that had an elastic band at the bottom. She covered her head with a colorful scarf embellished with colorful pom-poms; and she wore a large piece of silver jewelry around her double chin neck.

Amia Zomia told his wife, Hortense, what he had heard in a whisper from the stone statue. "The stone statue has an aura intrigue of mystery," he said.

"Did you hear any names?" Hortense asked.

"The stone statue whispered the name Shipoopi in my ear," said Amia Zomia.

Hortense shivered with a death grip of chilling cold in her spine as she heard the name Shipoopi. "Oh, thunder," she said. "Did you hear any other names?"

"The stone statue whispered a snake-woman. Shipoopi is a snake-woman."

"Is there any other names?"

"No other names, just the snake-Shipoopi."

"I see sore and silent stone statue. I see rather treacherous. I will see to it in due time."

"Thank you for going to bat for me," he said. "I'm glad you are on my team."

"Where else would I be!" she said. "I will see to it in due time."

Days passed, nights passed, Hortense was unable to gain a sensory contact with a woman named Shipoopi. Days passed and nights rolled in like ocean tides, and there were still no signs of clairvoyance "clear seeing" allowing her to visualize Shipoopi. One specific night, while the moon was hovering in the shadowy black sky the clairvoyant Hortense looked-up at the moon and saw a monstrous figure—a female creature with a head of hair consisting entirely of snakes. She saw a monster figure in the reflecting moon, which had grotesquely foreshortened her.

Hortense sat with a fearful shock while she was contemplating the horror figure on the surface of the bright moon, and said, "It is something out of the depths of hell."

Her husband placed a hand on her shoulder, and said, "Can you handle it?"

"I am afraid that I can't handle it. This is too much for me to bear."

"I know of a person who can help out," he said. "He goes by the name Garbanzo."

Jerry Garbanzo was commended for his valor actions. He was eighty-two-year-old heroic-man, six feet tall. His wrinkled oval face reflected a roadmap of his own life experiences. He took a vow to abstain from marriage and lived a life of mystery; and he faithfully lived up to his vow. He had a remarkably prescient vision—powers to see the unseen world and the ability to communicate with it. He dressed himself in a short sleeve white shirt, baggy white trousers, and a white bobble cap. His worn flat sandals were made out of goat skin. He lived all his days on the extreme edge of the village in a two-room shack.

The following evening Amia Zomia visited Jerry Garbanzo. Garbanzo requested to be fully informed so he could make a rational decision.

"What did your wife, Hortense, actually see?" Garbanzo said.

"You know my wife is a clairvoyant, she can see only certain images. She told me that she saw a monstrous image reflected in the moon—a female creature having a head of hair intertwining with snakes."

"Did she see her eyes?"

"She told me that her eyes were shut while the snakes were coiling and dancing from her crown."

Garbanzo muttered nervously, "This is mind-boggling stuff!" He was overly-heated and was sweating like a porous pitcher. "Gee willikers," he said. "Hmm, tell me what you heard from the stone statue?"

"I am a clairaudient as you know, I hear what is inaudible. I heard that he was transformed to a stone statue by his wife."

"It is mind-boggling stuff!"

"You are the right man for the stuff!"

"Did the stone statue reveal his wife's name?"

"Shipoopi; describing her as a snake-woman."

"It is mind-boggling stuff!"

"You have the knowledge of the prescience."

"Can you describe the stone statue to me?"

"It is a full-length figure of a man, made of stone."

"A man trapped in stone, huh?"

"I was sad to hear his story."

Garbanzo whispered nervously, "There is unseen danger from her, Shipoopi. It is mind-boggling stuff."

Garbanzo asked Amia Zomia to shift himself to another room where he would make a direct contact with the imperceptible world.

They entered cautiously into the room. Everything was utterly dark inside. Nothing was visible clearly to Amia Zomia. Garbanzo lit up a single candle and placed it in its holder. Suddenly something appeared at the room's door then quickly blew the door shut. The room was engulfed with a frigid air with the smell of manure. They sat on an old tattered floor mat located in the middle of the dimly lit room. The moonlight filtered in through a hole in the ceiling and gleamed down on a rounded metal tub full of water. They sat in a circle around the metal tub. With each gesture, something came to Garbanzo's rugged hands, as if he anticipated each catch—he was catching a floating garbanzo beans like a baseball catcher at home-base. Then he tossed each garbanzo bean into the water while he was examining the after effects of the water riddles. He had a coarse manner of speech while was screaming raggedly and demanding "Shipoopi" to appear before him. Then, like a magical spell, something stirred the water and that something was the reflection of a woman with snakes covered her head in the eerie-murky water. They veered away from the water tub as the water was making an ominous rattling sound; and departed from the room.

Garbanzo shook his sweaty head. "It is mighty mind-boggling stuff, enough to melt hell!" he said. "Who is she? From where did she slither out from?"

"She is the snake-woman; who my wife saw," Amia Zomia said.

"She is from Hell! That's where she is from."

"Can you hunt and destroy her?"

"Never underestimate the power of goodness; It is the strongest power you can imagine."

"I'd be obliged to you."

"The buck stops here."

"Thank you, Garbanzo, and good-night." He left satisfyingly.

That same night Garbanzo heard a voice in his dream: "The monster's head has nine snakes with nine lives. For every snake severed off, the monster will regrow two more snakes. You can kill nine snakes only under the full moon . . . a mirror and sword, a mirror and sword.

The monster discovered you and your friend and his wife; the monster will seek revenge on the three of you. Kill the monster, kill the monster, you must kill the monster!" Then he visualized a vision of a monster's head attached with nine snakes under a quicksand.

According to ancient times Shipoopi was Sledge's first wife. When a full moon was hovering over the sky, Sledge thought that Shipoopi would submit to him, but she refused to do so, instead she would make herself scarce—under a full moon she refused to lie down under Sledge during sex and eventually became bored of him. As she transformed to a snake woman; the gaze from her black marble eyes turned all who dared to glance at her to stone. As for Shipoopi, she was chasing her next prey of a husband, and they all had the same fateful blueprint as Sledge under the bewitching spell of a full moon. A devil called Moonercan had lived in the moon since ancient times. It was his reflection in the full moon that would transform Shipoopi into a snake-woman. She was one of his collections!

One overly full moon night, the meticulous plan was finalized and was nothing but an implementation. That night, both Jerry Garbanzo and Amia Zomia were on the same page of an act of killing Shipoopi. When they finally arrived at Shipoopi's property it was well past midnight. Jerry Garbanzo was carrying a sword in one hand hiding it under his long black shirt and a mirror in the other hand; Amia Zomia was holding a mirror and gunny sack.

Shipoopi's shack was located just thirty minutes away from Garbanzo's place. Her shadowy place was darkly shrunken from the rest of the world, deliberately to be invisible. It resembled an abandoned-condemned dwelling as it had chosen solitude over society. The obsolete house was no more than a shack on its last legs of a foundation. Against the night lit sky, Garbanzo and Amia Zomia could only see the crumbling exterior, which were nothing more than a ghostly silhouette of some long-ago era. The two windows of the shack looked like an empty-searching souls, along with the once grand door at the entryway of the shack which seemed to provide the impression it was an entrance, escorting one to Hell. The weather-faded green wooden door and the two faded green windows were completely covered with thick layers of dust with mildew that looked like it has been intentionally untouched for years. The night air near the shack was as cold as ice enough to make one's teeth chatter; and it was engulfed with a repulsive-stench of rotten eggs.

They walked barefooted across the sand toward the ominous shack—they were treading quietly and cautiously. When they approached the shack's door, they eyed the place carefully and then stood gapping at each other. Garbanzo cleared away the dirt that was blocking a small opening through the door with his hand and stared behind-beyond the entrance of the shack's door. He saw nothing but stark dark of the inside tomb of the repulsive shack. Garbanzo signaled Amia Zomia to stay vigilant by the frame of the door, while he was standing with a great deal of caution with attentiveness by the other frame. Silence prevailed, seconds scaled over, and time began, as if it was standing still.

The snake-haired Shipoopi tended to avoid all physical contact with Spud and Spade during the two/three full-moon nights; she deliberately locked them out, and making them camp out at Pojangles' shrine during those moonlit nights. It was a part of their monthly routine. On that particular moonlit night, the snake-haired Shipoopi sensed a series of scratches and a sharp intake of breath outside her main door, while she was rambling about the nooks and crannies of her shack. At that moment in time the shack was making a peculiar rattling noise and creaking sound. Their expressions seemed troubled and their legs were trembling with fear as the rattling noise and the creaking sound were quite clear to them.

Amia Zomia leaned over and whispered in Garbanzo's ear, "Hearing rattling and creaking sounds inside!"

Garbanzo whispered back, "So am I, keep quiet and watch the two windows; remember to look only at her reflection in the mirror."

Every door may be shut but death's door. Slowly the main door was pulled open with a squeaky creak; a head with venomous snakes in place of hair peeped out slowly from behind the door. The head twisted, turning toward Garbanzo. A demon face was reflected in the mirror—an evil face with fair complexion was glowing with a golden-brown tint with vast array of snakes held on her head. The swaying and rattling snakes held on her head were flopping over white eyes that copied vampire's eyes. A forked tongue as a carpet python tongue was twisting from a wide-open mouth, surrounded by long sharp shredding teeth as piranha's teeth. The two men performed courageously in staying calm with the frightening appearance of a monster-head until Garbanzo had been swift with his sword; he swung the sword at the pudgy neck with all his strength as he captured the neck reflection in his mirror. He was able to cut off the head of the monster at the doorway of the shack. At age of sixty, she was beheaded by Jerry Garbanzo. The severed snake-haired head, which once had the domination of turning the victims into stone, all who dared to look upon it, was lying lifeless at the doorway.

The reflection of the severed snake-haired head and torso of Shipoopi on their mirrors were horrific; and made them shuddered with horror. The snakes which existed on the severed head coiled up while they were hissing maliciously at Garbanzo; then lifted their demonic heads and died while the headless torso was gushing blood as a roman fountain. The headless torso then slumped on the floor of the doorway—it was the woman's torso. They carefully guided themselves by their mirrors toward the severed snake-haired head of Shipoopi, which retained its evil spell to turn onlookers to stone; and it was disposed at last in the gunny sack. They shut the door of the shack behind the torso and scurried away with the severed snake-haired head.

That same night/early morning Garbanzo and Amia Zomia buried the severed snake-haired head—they buried it deep in the sand, beyond retrieval. The darkness suddenly faded out, leaving them in light. Hortense's heart was released from her throat when she heard the news from Amia Zomia. Garbanzo was mightily relieved to see himself back safely in his own place.

Later, the prescient Jerry Garbanzo described the mortal Shipoopi as a beauteous fallen woman who seduced men and couldn't keep her stubby legs closed inside the shrine of Pojangles. She was well known of her nefarious activities inside the sacred place of Pojangles. Such a sacrilege attracted the Pojangles' wrath; he punished her by turning her hair to snakes; and all her cur husbands to a stony death.

The following day, most of the village dwellings were covered by sand except Pojangles' shrine, Garbanzo's and Amia Zomia's places. What actually transpired there? Why the village that once inhabitable was then covered in sand? No one had a single clue of the lost-locked-mystery, except Jerry Garbanzo, Amia Zomia, and Hortense. They believed in the supernatural force of Pojangles; he was the only one who had the power over the vastness of the desert landscape; he signaled the end of Shipoopi and signaled it was time to vacate. The shack of Shipoopi was completely vanished from the face of the earth with her torso, along with five stone statues of her aging low-level assortment of husbands: Bin Ben, Bongo, Bingo, Bubbles, and Bolero. The locale where her severed snake-haired head was buried turned into endless depth of a quicksand-grave. Like a useless broken timepiece of lost time she was never discovered. The village was consumed by nightly hauntings of the ghostly new-residents, giving free rein to its living habitants to abandon their modest dwellings in order to escape the supernatural wrath. Without will or conscious control, everyone abandoned the village, including Jerry Garbanzo, Amia Zomia and his wife, Hortense; leaving behind the Shrine and the statue of Sledge Shishbani as witnesses of the past.

After the door was unlocked to her horrific secret, Spud and Spade Shishbani froze the nightmarish memories of their mother from their lives. At the age of twenty-five, they departed for another place without uttering a word with the blessing of Pojangles, and that turned out to be a blessing in disguise.

The houses that were once inhabited were then all swallowed by the desert sand, and the place became surrounded by the presence of an eerie silence, since. The site remained abandoned and lived as a ghost residence for many of years. According to the nearby locals, the place was inhabited by a devil and holy man—a snake-haired head woman was called Shipoopi and a holy man named Pojangles. They believed that the holy man applied his holy spells to support and protect anyone who was willing to destroy her. The locals believed that she was beheaded by a valorous man named Garbanzo; and her snake-haired head was buried under the sand, but still had a potent force to turn anyone who sees it to stone. The place was known by some locals nearby as "Shipoopi Sands" and "Pojangles' Grave" by others.

The elderly couple, Amia Zomia and Hortense, resided together a few years in a nearby village close to Jerry Gabanzo, and they all chose never to venture back to that horrifying place. They lived in obedience to Pojangles, and dwelled too much in the past. They passed away peacefully, with the comfort of perceiving that Pojangles would be welcoming the trio, on the other side of the upward doorway. Amia Zomia and Hortense lived as one and died as one; he died at age of eighty, and she died at age of ninety. Garbanzo passed on later at age of ninety-two.

It was a metaphorical story that symbolized a she-devil as a shape of a human. The story was a fountain of belief mixed with courage which inspired nearby locals about a visionary figure and three strong-willed people who confronted and killed a disciple of Satan named Shipoopi. The metaphorical story behind the slaying of Shipoopi on her doorway would find its place among the other literal stories of that type.

In a world of clairvoyance, there was a young man named Pojangles who searched for the doors of ambition and knowledge. He travelled to the ends of the earth and was fascinated by all the deserts. At the end he settled in an oasis in a faraway desert. He developed a practice for clairvoyance there, and married a woman of the desert named Cactus Split. Then the disputes arose between him, his wife and her relatives; they accused him of being a warlock, which was punishable by death in the law of that oasis. One night he took off leaving behind Cactus Split and her judgmental relatives. After that, he settled in another oasis, progressing in the upper levels of the clairvoyance, which prompted him to be preoccupied with the clairvoyant-hood. He was yearning to be transformed into a donkey, to expose the reality of people. He became a unique donkey. As a donkey he moved from one place to another, while observing closely at the inhumanity of the humans. He wished not to be a human again, and his wish became true. Clairvoyant sources did not specify his end, except to indicate that he died in his prime as a donkey. Some greater power succeeded in returning him to his human form in his grave. That was the abstract of the clairvoyant known as Pojangles.

Shishbani

Yesterday is today's memory, casts a shadow on the wall of the past; tomorrow is today's dream, and casts an anchor on the other shore of reality. Behind all the glitter, a memory in the real life can be unbearable. Some memories are roses, they are rare to find and bring them back; and some are just sharp thorns imbedded and stuck in the hearts, they are hard to forgive and forget them. Some memories can be shared and some can be trouble to be shared. A memory has an endless life compared to the nine lives myth of a cat.

Joseph had a very strong sentimental attachment to where he grew up. His memory kept a diary—he reminisced about his childhood and adolescent days. Some past places remained unchanged and had a deep intimacy/animosity with his innermost existence, whispering in pairs, good and bad, to him. It was difficult for Joseph to locate the eraser to his bad memories. His future was reeled back and found himself pining for the past. Later in life, he had no regrets nor did he puzzle over life in general and felt satisfied, for most of the time, to live in his inquisitive past. All places had resided in the child's mind as they were.

His seventy square foot bedroom was his private space; it contained a small brown cabinet closet for hanging his clothes, small bookcase, studying desk with a chair and lamp. The child's bedroom was situated at the end of the eastside of the living room. His bedroom was a small-scale room, cold in the winter and warm in the summer. He used his own method of meditation to adapt himself to the extreme degrees of temperatures in his small room.

His bedroom was known by the family as the "broken room" and its name was given by his Mother Lima. The broken room was a food storage unit for the family, before his mother gave her permission and consent to be used as his own bedroom. The broken room was a storage venue for: Edam, Parmesan and cheddar cheese, virgin olive oil, green and black olives, tomato paste, canned tuna in olive oil, red hot and black peppers, turmeric, cumin, a long thin spaghetti, white and brown flour, rice, dried kidney and white beans, dried lima beans, dried peas and a stock of dried lamb meat in olive oil in a big pottery container, kitchen utensils, small and large rugs and mats. Most of the food stored in the broken room was Italian brand.

Joseph was surprised to discover he was perfectly capable to meditate in order to relax and enhance his listening and focusing skills. His meditation went beyond where he lived—at the age of eight he began to discover what was going on beyond his bedroom window; that would be one index card from his past.

One spring afternoon, while the child was meditating at the ceiling of his bedroom and deeply relaxed on his twin bed, he heard a noise coming from outside through his second-floor window. The noise was a mixture of strange and scary rhythms, which interfered with his afternoon meditation. He jumped out of his bed, rushed to the window and peeked down through the blind slats to see what the hullabaloo was about. He was shocked and frightened for what he had seen! He saw something like a palm tree with limps and an odd-wobbling-head, dancing in the middle of the street below, in front of the three-story building where he resided. The lead dancer wrapped his entire body with fibers of the proliferating palm tree, and was decorated with an assortment of sea and land snails, and he also wore a turban and mask of the same fibers. His feet were covered with palm tree fibers. He was accompanied and encircled by balding men with ponytails acting as ensemble dancers; they were all in long white shirts and trousers. The lead dancer and the ensemble were all in festive/carnival mood. The scene became a hodgepodge of words and dialects, some from the lead dancer, and some from the ensemble. The six feet high lead dancer was jumping as a grasshopper while his barefooted ensemble danced around him. The ensemble jumped up and down like toads in a thunderstorm, leaping for joy when they saw the lead dancer's style of dancing was rather unique, as a popcorn kernel on a hot plate, technique. Their behavior was a world that coheres through animal connection rather than humans. They suddenly appeared as if by magic underneath Joseph's window, and began to shout, "Shishbani," a name that suggested it would be for the lead dancer. The rest of the street was just bystanders; and they all laughed loudly when the Shishbani changed to new dance moves. The Shishbani was dancing while the ensemble chanted an ode to him, in a high, wavering pitch:

Shishbani is Pojangles in disguise
O Shishbani, you're so wise
He went over the moon
To see what he could see
He saw Satan Moonercan
Holding Shipoopi Moonercan
Shishbani is Pojangles in disguise
O Shishbani, you're so wise
He stuck his head in a cave
To see what he could see
He saw a light without flame
The face of Pojanles he claim
Shishbani is Pojangles in disguise
O Shishbani, you're so wise
He travelled across the days of old
To see what he could see
He saw Garbanzo on the legends platform
With Amia plus Hortense in their best form

The ensemble seized from chanting for Shishbani to chant an ode to the bygone village:

Oh my heart
Don't ask where the village was gone
It was a monument built of illusion

So it collapsed in the crack of dawn
Fill my cup and drink to its allusion
How that village now be on the timeline
Just a mere whisper on the lips of time
That village becomes news
From the air talks so misuse

When Shishbani felt exhausted, the chorus waved their heads slowly in a sense of incoherence, and concluded with an ode to Shishbani:

Shishbani hey pani
This is his state and shape
There is no hide nor escape
Of his descendant of Spade
He felt shame in the shade
Shishbani hey pani
This is his state and shape
Spud twin brother to Spade
He was took and slowly fade
And no spuders were made
Shishbani hey pani
This is his shape and state
He opened his own life-gate
We wept over his sad fate
Tear-drops will not return his state
He returned
He returned from the shrub
And the full-moon lit up
Don't deprive your kindness to us
Which is the best gift to us
You are on our side
Every whisper beside
Every touch glide
A thousand candles of love

Enlightened in our hearts from above
Shishbani hey pani
This is his state and shape

Joseph pondered about the strange world of these people, a world that had ceased to be forever. His mind twitched away from the imagination pursuit; he knew it was true. Then his mother suddenly appeared in his bedroom doorway. "Mother . . . who are those men down there?" he asked.

"Pay them no mind," she said.

"Who are 'they'?"

"They belong way back. They belong to different time, different era. They are less civilized to what we are accustomed to living now."

"They are a scrambled mixture of mumbo jumbo."

"Yes, they have; they are looking for any hand-outs."

"Like what?"

"Like a bunch of garbanzos, beans, or some cash."

"That's new technique, huh?"

"Sort of—" she paused, then left his room. She was thirty-one years of age, five feet two inches tall; petite, with black short hairstyle; dressed herself in brightly colored dresses. Her vibrant hazel-eyes were clear and alert; and she was known for her savvy and strong management skills. She had a fifty-four-year-old husband, Jonah, and three children: Kareem, Joseph, and Freddie; nine, eight, and two years old, respectively.

The ensemble started shouting, "Go, go; go, Shish go; go, go"; while Shishbani was dancing for the jargon. Then they began to beat on their empty tin cans, while Shishbani was hopping like a kangaroo and ululating like a grieving widower. He paused to rest then pointed to his head, signaling for the ensemble to beat on their baldheads. They began to beat on their empty heads, while he was performing a head-spin—rotating on his head like a wooden spinning top.

Joseph stood behind the window, watching their every movement and listening with undivided attention. Suddenly, Shishbani sprung to his feet, stretched and glimpsed up. He sensed a peeping spectator from a certain window toward him. He quickly revealed his face and it was covered by leprosy; then he peered up, and frowned back at the window. When Shishbani flared his face and his bulging eyes, Joseph quickly stepped away from the window. He rushed out of his bedroom toward the main door of the apartment to make sure the main door was bolted. Then he returned back to his bedroom and took an extra precaution of locking his door. He stood at the window and lowered the wood blind, leaving a tiny gap between the slats, so he could bear witness what was happening down on the street.

The clamor reined to a slower pace, paused, and then they all lounged around the main door of the building except Shishbani. Joseph felt a growing sense of alarm when he realized how calm the intermission had become. He sensed that the creepy Shishbani, could have blood of a spider, to creep up the stone wall toward his window. Maybe, Shishbani wasn't so squeaky clean after all; maybe he was a crocodile from extinction lurking around on its webbed hind feet; a lizard without its tail basking in the heat of the afternoon sun; or maybe he was an imposter, who masqueraded as Shishbani. He carefully sussed out the situation and realized right away that Shishbani was just a lizard-like clown with the ability to glide walls. His mind was swirling around and around in a whirlpool of hallucination in which he thought a lizard was chasing after him. He left the window and went to check underneath his twin sized bed, desk, and his chair. He searched through his closet and bookcase, searching for the elusive lizard. He became more vigilant, stood up in the middle of his bedroom, and tuning his ears to the lizard channel; he stayed tuned until his ears picked up a strange swishing sound at his bedroom door.

"It's me, Joseph, Kareem."

No reply came from Joseph as he was bewildered by the continuous clicking sound behind his door. He thought the lizard was mimicking his brother.

"Are you okay?"

Joseph responded with silent stares.

"Cat got your tongue, huh?"

"Damn you, scram." Joseph responded in a quavering voice.

"I don't give a damn. Open the door!"

"Go away, you stupid lazy lizard."

"Who are you calling a stupid lizard?"

"You; you are nothing but a lizard."

"Okay, okay, have it your way. Open the door."

"Go chase a grasshopper."

"Now, you are talking fiddlesticks."

Lima heard Kareem exchanging words with Joseph. She came to the door side. Kareem whispered, "Joseph, by golly, open the door; your mother is here. You know she got a short fuse."

"Go away lazy lizard!"

"I heard what you've said. What in thunder is that?" Lima said angrily.

"You are the lizard's sidekick, aren't you?" Joseph said wearily.

She pondered for a moment before replying. "Who is the 'lizard'?"

"You are!"

"Open the door now, you stiff-necked billy goat."

"He thinks everyone is a lizard. He is kooky," Kareem said.

"Yeah, that's great. Everyone is a lizard, that's great," Lima said.

For a moment Joseph thought he was having hallucinations—he thought the lizard was performing his last bag of tricks on him, and his brother and mother were being held hostage by the lizard. Then, somehow, he brought out the fear in him and managed to regain his mental balance, when he realized that she was his mother who was speaking to him; he knew exactly what to expect from her. "I, um—," he paused.

"Open the door," Lima said. "I never repeat myself twice."

"Please, open the door, huh?" Kareem said.

Lima turned to Kareem, "Don't horn in."

"Yes, Mother."

"Stop yanking my chain, little squirt! Let me give you a word of warning; either you open the door, or I break it on your head." Lima said to Joseph.

When Joseph heard the "either-or" command; he knew very well there were consequences of disobeying her commands. She was a delivery drill sergeant when it came to her orders; she never went back on her words. He reloaded his discharged courage as quickly as he could, and walked cautiously toward the door; then he unlocked the door and hid behind it.

Lima and Kareem entered the bedroom, while Joseph was hiding behind the door. She yanked him by his arm, and walloped him on the derriere. "You little squirt," she said, "don't ever get impertinent with me, you little squirt."

Despite the painful spanking, he was relieved from his trauma. He muttered nervously, "Sorry, Mother."

"Sorry, my foot . . . you don't have one respectable bone in your body, little squirt."

He began to beg as the pace of slapping on his buttocks was intensifying. "Please, Mother, don't—"

"Don't what, little squirt."

He stuttered anxiously, "There is something I need to tell you, Mother." His bare legs trembled. "Oh, Mother," he said. "You are hurting me."

She continued with her walloping, "You got a lizard in your brain." Her anger appeared in her salty voice. "Little squirt," she said. "Calling me a lizard, huh, is that so."

"I am sorry, Mother."

She slapped his face quite hard; and pushed him away over the edge of his bed. She had a little too much bloodhound in her for the interrogation. "Why did you lock yourself inside your room; calling everyone a lazy lizard including me?"

"I was afraid—" he paused abruptly.

"Afraid of what?—"

"I . . . I . . ."

"Cut it out; afraid of what!"

"I was afraid he wants to hunt me!"

"Who is 'he'?"

"The lizard—"

"Ick, a lizard was chasing you!"

"To kill me—"

"Big-time fool; where is it?"

"I don't know. It just is."

"Where did you see it; speak up."

"I thought—"

"'I thought' is not an answer. Where is the lizard?"

"I thought he would come from underneath the door."

"I wonder."

"Thought is the seed of action, Mother."

"Your answer is as clear as mud."

The chanting of the ensemble with Shishbani slowly faded in the distance, until all that remained were the echoes of their presence and the occasional sounds from the watchers. "Aw, good riddance," she said.

"I watched them from my window. The one they call him 'Shishbani' glared up, staring at me until I became frightened," Joseph said.

"Tell me your story once again!"

He said cautiously, "I am not storying you, Mother."

"You storied me!"

He knew that he had to confront his fears. "I never lied to you. I was scared I felt a little bit foolish."

It was then that Kareem intervened. "Who isn't scared of Shishbani? I was scared too."

"They are just rats in the corner," Lima said.

"Who is this 'Shishbani'?" Joseph said.

She came (at length) to the window, on which there was no Shishbani to be seen, "Rat in the corner." Her anger openly disappeared. "Oh, my sons," she said. "I've been known to tell the truth cold sober all of the time."

"I love you, Mother," said Joseph.

"The very same to all of you," she said, "if something I did or said can be interpreted in two ways, and one of those ways had upset you, then I meant the other one!" She walked out of the room, closing the door as she left.

Joseph turned to Kareem, "I feel a little bit foolish."

"You are not. I can scent the imagination of your mind. I do feel you have a talent for imagination. One day you will use your imaginative talent when writing stories," Kareem said.

"Really, you mean that!"

"Sure enough I mean it." Kareem left the room.

Joseph later found the key to writing—he kept the imagination flowing from the ink of his pen onto the paper of his writings.

There was once upon a time, in a village far, far away, a man named Bud Bones, the descendant of Spade Shishbani; he moved to a town, where he met his wife, Loonet. After their only son, Scorp, was murdered (someone sliced his throat from ear-to-ear in some barbershop); Bud Bones was insistent to bury him in the ground of his ancestors, land of Shipoopi, despite the constant warnings of Loonet's visions of Shipoopi. Scorp returned as a zombie slayer—returned to life as a killer-walker corpse.

Bud Bones had a vision that Pojangles granted him three wishes, and when he woke up from his sleep, he revealed his vision to his wife, Loonet. She demanded him to use the first wish on her—to be the most stunning woman in the world. He used the first wish and she did become the most beautiful woman in the world. When she became the most beautiful woman in the world, she ditched him. Bud Bones shouted vengefully, "O, Pojangles, turn Loonet into an old lame sow, please." That evening he saw an old lame sow with a woman's head at his shack, pleading with him; so he shouted vengefully back again, "O, Pojangles, turn Loonet into a lizard, please." She came back as half-and-half, half-lizard and half-woman.

If Bud Bones had let his wife, Loonet, have her own-vain way, after consuming the first wish, he would have been able to use the other two wishes to return the frigid-stiff Scorp back to life, and provide them with abundance of wealth. But he chose the dead end highway for revenge and lost his wife and son altogether. Bud Bones disowned

Scorp, the zombie; because of his peculiar appearance and bizarre behavior. The zombie's body was covered with leprosy; and his brain was transformed into a lizard-brain. That's where it ends, Bud Bones of love; Bud Bones of wrath.

To Bud Bones only the past was real; there was no present; and his future was filled with uncertainty and fear. He was friendless, self-absorbed in the hellish memories of Loonet and Scorp, until one night, and it was a fateful night for him, when he discovered something strange lying next to him under the cover in his bed. A creature with the head and upper body of a beautiful young woman and the tail of a lizard was lying right next to him. Although he couldn't see all of her physique, he recognized her straight off—she was none other than loony Loonet. Immediately, he felt something warm and slimy over his legs; he thought for a moment that she peed on him. He sprang up rapidly, snatched the cover off her, and stooped swiftly over her body. A crocodile lizard tail fluttered toward him, trying to strangle him. He barely escaped being caught by the mammoth tail. On the double, he swung his meaty fists against the croc-lizard tail, hurriedly moved back and darted from the room with the suit he was born with. Then he ran stark naked to a nearby palm tree and lay down to hide from loony Loonet.

While the croc-lizard-tailed Loonet was having a limited amount of mobility in the bed, she heard a hissing sound from outside the bedroom. She was stone-cold scared; she reflected for a moment, a hisser was slithering eagerly toward her. At first she thought of a snake, and every thought in her mind was that some snake was after her for its next prey. Suddenly, the sound of hissing packed the bedroom; she felt a prickling sensation down her tail, grabbed her tail up, but she soon realized there was nothing she could do to keep the predator from afar. The hisser continued to hiss with the gnashing of teeth and gasping for air. Every high-pitched hiss from the hisser made a foul sound in her ears. She then observed something odd outside, like a ghostly silhouette flickering in the dark, and heard a groan of dismay and shuffling feet which made her croc of a tail trembling like a tree branch in the wind. The shuffling sound continued and then ceased right behind her bedroom door. Her thought process was shattered when she heard the door-knocks, and was beyond frightened; she jumped off the bed onto the floor, nearly severed ties with her tail. *"It might be him, Bud Bones, the murderer!" she said.* A raspy-screech echoed from outside, "Who's there"? She freaked out. "Who's this?" she said. He moaned as a zombie, "Scooorp." Neither he nor it he was. The half-it and half-he corpse then shoved the door wide open. She thought she knew who the moaner was; but the moaner showed her that the real zombie was in a place she never expected—her bedroom. She shouted and bawled out for help, but there was no one nearer her but the awaiting zombie. As the stiff was shuffling in, she squeaked, roared, and bawled like some dying animal, crying out in pain with its last breath, groveling on the floor in fear; then she lay on the bloody floor as a corpse, barely breathing at all.

The zombie came out from the death-bedroom and froze in the doorway, gripping Loonet'a upper-half body in one hand and a lizard's tail in the other hand. The zombie's hands were stained with blood; and the rest of its body was covered in mud. It had black deadpan eyes, and a mouth dripping with blood. Nothing in its body was coordinated, its right hand was shorter than its left; and its left leg was one foot longer than its right. Its lips had been chewed off, perhaps that was a kiss from a senior zombie that converted him into a zombie. The zombie growled. "I sliced you into halves, Bitch. And that's what you are and what you deserve. I'll butcher that son of a bitch, Bud Bones, when I get my paws on him." The zombie threw its hands up, throwing the two halves onto the ground; then shuffled its awkward feet and departed from the shack.

There in the heart of the desert stood a sacred palm tree, its bark was so perfectly patterned as if it was carved out by a sculptor. The grand palm tree stretched up, as if it was so proud to stand there under the sun in any season; and it was a refuge from the darkness of the world. That night the tall palm tree sensed that someone was holding its trunk—that someone was none other than Bud Bones, who was quivering with horror from his mutant wife, the lizard-tailed Loonet. When the blessed palm tree sensed what was approaching; it lifted its crown toward the sky and requested an offering. Momentarily, a light was dappling through its ample leaves, and fell across Bud Bones' mug. He looked up at the sky and spent few seconds gazing at something which caught his eye—a white-winged human was hovering in the sky. The human-bird hybrid descended gradually from the sky, and then disappeared. When Bud Bones peeked, he saw a man in his undergarments with a long white beard and two large milky-wings was actually sitting with his back against the palm tree. And then he witnessed the avian-humanoid looking up at the crown of the palm tree and his lips began to move. All of a sudden, the crown of the tree began to shake and quiver, dropping its soft leaves with ease on the bare body of Bud Bones. The leaves were covered with a strange sticky substance; and by happenstance he was covered from head to toe with the soft-sticky leaves. Then all at once the winged-man vanished in a split second, like he some sort of spook.

After the winged man had vanished from the scene, lightning flashed across the sky. All at once, the looming dust storm rolled over the earth and right on cue a light began to fall haphazardly from the sky, as if it was committed to the plan of protecting Bud Bones. The floating dust in light immediately blanketed Bud Bones and mercifully edged him away from Scorp, the zombie. There was no sign of Bud Bones under the palm tree, other than the dust-light. Howling gusts of wind grew louder and louder, trying with its speedy-strength to lift Scorp, the zombie. The dust devil seemed to lift up the zombie as a fallen feather, clutching it briefly, and then blew it away. Scorp was transported by the dust devil to the land which had a motto, "He who unleashes the terror, reaps the terror". The new locale was the land of madness due to the eerie noises echoing at night, as a result of the wind gust striking the zombies. It was beyond the land-of-no-return; it was Shipoopi's land.

The egg yolk sun poured through the gaps in the palm leaves and awaited the entrance into Bud Bones' eyes. When the sun settled above the horizon, radiating light; he hesitantly rubbed the remainders of the nightmares from his eyes and gazed up at the sky. The new day welcomed Bud Bones like a long-lost bosom friend. But it wasn't a friendly day, because he never felt that way before—he felt the warmth had been siphoned from his heart; and his memory had floated away from him, like a leaf being pulled away in the tide, and submerged. He woke up as if it was an emergency, clinging to the very last mental image from the night before without success. His body was covered from head to toe with fronds, every inch of his body was aching; he was in so much agony from his new attire, the embedded-leaves. He stood up and turned around; he was shocked by his physique—he had sticky leaves embedded to his birthday suit; and his entire body was sculptured to perfection as a sapling palm tree, instantly giving off the impression that he popped up from a young palm. The fronds-covered Bud Bones resembled a miniature replica of a palm tree. The pain crushed him—it left him incapable of anything. With fearful suffering, he turned to the palm tree, begging for mercy, and said, "Please, pluck off your fronds; they are very painful." The palm tree replied, "You need to soft-pedal your pain if you want to win over your pain. Take the pain of gain; all wise men can, can't you?" After a while the pain faded away, and he became half-man and half-palm tree. His whole body was covered with fronds, and his hands looked like two branches of a palm. He had a sapling palm tree look with an itchy bare feet.

Bud Bones, the half-man and half-palm, began to wander from one place to another, from one village to another, where people tended to avoid all physical contact with him. His appearance scared off everyone, especially the children. One day he settled down in an abandoned place, half an hour's walk from a neighboring village. In order to provide for his day-to-day needs; he began to go to that village, begging for pity and some change from any passerby. On one occasion, he met a man named Lootie who was a proprietor of a nearby traveling-carnival. Lootie offered half-Bud Bones and half palm a job in his carnival, encouraging him to take full advantage of his body deformities and performing in stage shows; and whoever wanted to watch his show will pay a pretty penny. The half-Bud Bones, half palm agreed and began performing in the carnival. Hence, his fame spread like wild fire to all the villages and towns as a carnival performer. The most famous newspapers interviewed him and wrote special feature articles about him, which caused his fame to skyrocket. Bud Bones, the half-man and half-palm, became an overnight global superstar—to view his act or even to take a picture with him would cost a small fortune.

How quickly Lootie's admiration flipped to jealousy—he allowed the green-eyed monster to devour him without the willingness to push on the brakes, and think the best of Bud Bones. His heart that was once filled with so much care and regard for Bud Bones was replaced with bitterness and malice. His envy didn't ebb, it multiplied. Lootie's wife T-Shred was stimulated by her husband's pure animosity toward Bud Bones, and seemed efficient enough for both to find a malicious method to unleash their enviousness assault on the unknowingly Bud Bones.

The path of their crime plot began to ascend more rapidly, day after day. One day T-Shred decided the time had come for the demise of Bud Bones. The paramount part of the plan was executed by her. When the light of that day drained away, they both blended away into the blackness of the night, and went straight to the carnival. They found Bud Bones standing alone inside the carnival. Lootie took a deep breath, and told Bud Bones that he and his wife knew about a procedure to get rid of the leaves that were embedded in his entire body. His sanctimonious and self-serving tone had pervaded Bud Bones' hearing. It was delightful news for Bud Bones to hear that there was such a mighty machine. Bud Bones was encircled in a bear-hug-style from behind by the arms of Lootie, and preceded by the overly pungent-perfumed scent of T-Shred; then ushered to a secluded site, far away from the carnival. Lootie curled his fingers around a big portable machine, which had a large rectangular in shape chamber, at one end and a curved stem with a hole at the other end. They reassured him that he was in good hands, and the machine would be ready in five minutes. They showed him where to lie and from where he would come out as a whole new person. Bud Bones' spirits lifted a few notches when he heard the talk and saw the machine; he showed no sign of apprehension; he was ready mentally and physically for the procedure. They took deep breath and lifted him up and lay him on the hopper, and then slid him head first into the center opening of the machine.

Lootie gave him a gentle push toward the feed chute, while T-Shred was groping for the start switch. Altogether, they started at the same time—she switched the machine on, while Lootie kept pushing and shoving Bud Bones' body inside the feed chute. A sudden eerie shriek pierced the silence, while the blades were gripping Bud Bones' head and his life's blood was gushing out like a river from the chute. The blood had smeared down Lootie's body as a butcher's block. He was blurred with blood, and couldn't see Bud Bones' legs. Bud Bones Shishbani was all shredded away by a tree shredder. Lootie had to feel for Bud Bones' feet, to make sure he had slipped through the blades. Then, he unconsciously misread his own action, trying to reach for Bud Bones' feet. It was too late for T-Shred to switch the machine off after Lootie's upper body had been spewed out by the grinder as mincemeat via the discharge chute of the tree shredder. She violently banged her head on the death-trap machine many times, whimpering with terror like a wounded-animal, and banging her hands hysterically on her hefty hips. She shockingly glanced at Lootie's half-severed body, and then darted off into the still of the night. Her mind was the kind of a demented mind that belonged to those not long for this world.

One day, she ended up in the land of Shipoopi. Luckily, she missed the quicksand of Shipoopi's head, but her lady-luck had run out its course when she didn't miss the welcoming party of Scorp, the zombie.

Doorway Four

Blind on Arrival

The Visit

The past has no existence in the present, it only exists in memory. Memory is the audio picture of the mind, like a video camera, of the five senses—sight, hearing, touch, smell and taste—when the mind is present. There are additional senses that accompany the standard five senses: the sense of loss, balance in life, motion, direction, and the sense of time. Also, there are other senses that develop throughout the childhood/adulthood, like sense of self-respect and respect toward others, sense of morals, sense of love versus hate, sense of humor (good, bad, dry, witty or remarkable), sense of mood (temper), sense of danger, and sense of life and death.

Yesterday will never return; today will never last; and tomorrow will be where it will be. You cannot suffer from the past or future, because they don't exist; what you are suffering is the memory of the past or the imagination of the future. Some gifted people have a supernatural power for the forthcoming events known as premonition/prediction. Premonition is a clairvoyant or clairaudient experience which resonates with the future, especially unpleasant events; and it has no connection with the main five senses. Prediction or forecast is a statement about the future, pleasant or unpleasant events.

The sixth sense—the awareness—is that part that keeps humans making better decisions about what is going to happen; it is aided by the standard senses and forecast good and bad occurrences in a fraction of a second. Those who believe in the sixth sense, it is their connection to the future. The sixth sense is not controlled by time, place and the rules of nature.

Animal senses are more intuitive and much more sensitive than human senses. Humans have developed complex machines and technology in order to be able to predict and sense natural disasters before they actually happen, such as earthquakes and hurricanes. On the other hand, animals appear to be wired in some way to predict natural disasters using their ambiguous sixth sense. Plants have senses towards environment—they are sensitive to oxygen, carbon dioxide, light, water, gravity, movement, sound, touch, and diseases. The planet, which we inhabit, has intangible senses, such as motion and gravity. Human senses are restricted and limited compared to the senses of animals, plants, and the universe as a whole.

Joseph's bedroom was a small scale of a room, and was situated at the end of the eastside of the living-room. He had been lying on his bed when a whisper entered his ears. He sat up in the bed, listening.

"You are Joseph, my friend, aren't you?"

"Who is this?" Joseph said alarmingly.

"And you are seven years old, now, right?"

"Who are you?"

"Answer me?"

He held his tongue.

"The box keeps all the answers."

He remained silent.

"No need my boy; I already have all the information about you."

"You aren't my invisible sister, are you?"

"No, I am not. I am just a box."

"What a name, Box!"

"Box is not my given name; my name is Candora. I have been recording your daily life events since you entered this world."

"Have you been spying on me?"

"I have been secretly observing you since birth."

"Tell me how you gathered my most inner secrets?"

"My secret-service agents are your senses; your eyes, ears, skin, nose, tongue, and your mind; they are all my loyal assistants!"

Candora said. "I'm your subconscious."

"Is that true?"

"It sure is."

"Do you watch and record everyone, huh?"

"Everyone has his own box."

"Are you going to watch me, then?" he said.

"Until you leave this world," she said. Her whisper quieted, and quickly ceased.

His brain had faded away like the morning dew. There was many details went through his head; for a moment he thought he had a little touch in his head.

Joseph's parents, Jonah and Lima, were married in a very quaint ceremony, with immediate family only; they began their married life living for a few months with Merriam, Jonah's mother, along with Eve, Jonah's sister. Aunt Eve was trice married woman, which was her luck of the dice lucky number, and had three sons and four daughters from three different husbands.

Joseph's widowed grandmother, Merriam, was elderly, eighty-plus years of age, five feet ten inches tall, and slim. Her once fair face was wrinkled with age, and she was infirm. Her general outfit consists of a mid-length dress, baggy silk trousers that have an elastic band at the bottom, and a scarf on her head. She inherited the house, properties, and farms from her mother—great-grandmother to Joseph. The house was located on the side of a stone quarry, and resembled a white Italian castle with its frontal emerald-door dead center. The floor of the house was made of marble, and had seven identical rooms. Merriam's room was overlaid with rugs of oriental design, and a bed with an elaborate mahogany headboard.

Sabrina the eldest daughter to Eve was very envious of Lima. Lima and Sabrina were completely different as day and night. Sabrina was homely and two years younger than Lima. Lima was then twenty years of age, five feet two inches tall, clean-limbed, an attractive face with silky white skin, and short black pixie hairstyle. Sabrina was eighteen years of age, five feet tall, chunky, a face of envy with premature-aging pale skin, and greasy out of place black hair. Lima's hazel eyes were illuminated by her strong personality, whereas anyone could see jealousy-stirred waves in Sabrina's nanny goat eyes. Lima was very fastidious about her personal hygiene, while Sabrina was lackadaisical and sloppy about her personal hygiene.

One day the green-eyed monster of jealousy erupted from Sabrina's ever gaping mouth that made an abrupt end for the topsy-turvy relationship between Sabrina and Lima. "You are constantly cleaning our kitchen and mopping the floor of our hall, you think we are not clean enough for you. Why you don't leave us be, if you think we are not perfectly as pure as you!" Sabrina told Lima. The acid-tongued, the jealousy-faced Sabrina, was not the type to go off without the motive of a confrontation.

The self-controlled Lima shrugged her shoulders and ignored the flashing signal of trouble waiting ahead.

That evening when Jonah returned back home, Lima made her point as clear as a bell. "I have seen and heard enough, in this house. I found your imperious niece, Sabrina, to be constantly rude and very truculent over my hygiene in this house," she said, "I want to move out, time's up for me."

"I know she could be impertinent," forty-three-year-old Jonah said. He despised Sabrina for the way she treated his wife.

"She is impossible."

"One of these days, her hatred will come back and haunt her."

"What goes around comes around."

Jonah and Lima moved to a more spacious residence, close by to Merriam's house. The apartment was very pleasing in appearance, had a stylish sense of charm, and it was on the second floor in a three-story building—one apartment on each floor. The wooden double front door of the building was as dark as the floor of a forest, tall as a redwood tree, and solid as a mountain. The double front door was usually halfway opened in the daytime and locked at nightfall. There was one marble step leading up to the doorway of the building. The main water valves and the main electrical panel box were located on the right side of the main entrance of the hallway. There were seven wide steps that led directly from the main hallway to the first apartment in the building. There was a wide wooden widow with marble sill on the first level, and was just about six feet off the floor. Another fifteen steps up, led into an open square area with a balcony jutted out from inside over the main door of the building. Jonah and Lima's apartment was located on the second floor, at the end of another staircase leading fifteen stairs up. There was a small rectangular area in front of the main door of their apartment with a sizeable glass window on the wall, facing the stairs, serving as a source of extra light during the daytime.

Finally, Lima was as free as a bird in its nest. The marble entrance hall of the apartment had a shiny surface and a substantial glass window with a marble sill facing the east side of the building. The old-fashioned kitchen, twelve feet long by ten feet wide, was located at the west-end of the apartment. It was equipped with outdated items: stove from the early forties, built-in counter with a marble sink, large kitchen cabinet, and with old-fashioned utensils. There was a sparse trace left of a vintage era style of how the kitchen was once designed. All of the kitchen's items would appeal today to a museum collector, somewhere! The kitchen had a medium-sized window next to the marble sink, facing the east. Lima didn't mind the vintage kitchen equipment as long as she was an earshot away from the clutches of Sabrina's acidity tongue. The bathroom was located at the south end of the apartment. The window of the bathroom was facing east; and its curtain was closed at all the times as a deterrent for peeping Toms. There were three bedrooms, living room, dining room, and one storage room—it later became the bedroom for Joseph. Jonah and Lima's master bedroom was located at the far left-side of the apartment and had two immense windows, one facing north, looking out over the sea, and the other facing west.

Joseph was the second child after his one-year-older brother, Kareem. When Joseph was six-year-old, his third brother, Freddie, was born. Joseph and Kareem were close in age, and to each other. Their features were quite similar—both were medium height, slim-built, intelligent faces with short black hair and precious brown eyes. Their dress style was identical—in the summer they dressed in gray shorts, and white T-shirts; in the winter they dressed in black slacks, and white long sleeve shirts with black pulled-over sweaters. They always wore tennis shoes, and they had well-trimmed haircuts.

One autumn afternoon while Joseph was standing against the wall, facing the penetrating sunlight through the glass window of the hall, he heard the familiar uncomfortable command. "Zozo, you are coming with me this afternoon to visit the Batnoon's family," his mother said. His nickname was Zozo, and no one dared to call him by his nickname except his mother.

"No, Mother, I feel like staying at home, take Kareem instead." Joseph said.

"No, you are going with me. I don't want to walk unaccompanied in the street."

"Please, Mother, I would like to stay here and finish my homework."

Her words rushed out like a fire hose. "No. You are coming with me, end of story."

He left the scene and went right away to his bedroom.

Her voice rolled in like a draft rolling underneath his bedroom door. "I have no time for nonsense. I am waiting for you, hurry up!"

He said nervously, "Okay, Mother I'll be ready in five minutes." He was unhappy. *"What can I do now?" he whispered. "She is an octopus."* He would rather be seen with his father than his mother in public—he detested the thought of having his mother near him in the open. He reluctantly dressed up in blue sea of sadness and left the main building with the forcible tentacles of his mother. It was so embarrassing escorting his mother in public, especially, if any of his peers spotted him with her.

"Ten minutes is the distance between our home and the Batnoon's abode," Lima said. "You are quiet as a mouse who is allergic to cheese, what is wrong with you?"

"Oh, nothing," Joseph muttered. He was trembling.

They passed by his parental grandmother's residence, which was located on the right side of the street to the Batnoon's abode. "Why are you shivering as a little furless squirrel in the cold?" Lima said.

"I am good."

A building as ancient as the ruins of the Roman Empire was located next door to his paternal grandmother's residence. The decayed remains of the building was a fearful locale to pedestrians, day and night—a large loose black dog was growling at all hours, acting as an armed guard for the old eyesore of a building. The front of the ancient dwelling was a war zone around the clock between any passerby and the alerted mongrel. Most of the residents never dared to complain about the dog, which remained an intriguing mystery, to its bum owner, Skye, alias Sepia, who hid out in the condemned building. There was no other solution with the demonic dog other than avoiding it, be prepared to take a powder, or face it with a stone. Joseph and his mother walked cautiously up the street toward the Batnoon's abode, departing the barking of the savage dog behind. "A barking dog is better than a sleeping lion," Lima said. "Dogs bark to express their emotions, don't be afraid of them, huh?"

"A dog's bark is worse than its bite!" Joseph said.

"How do you know?"

"How should I know? I never have been bitten by a dog."

"Dog bite is worse than its bark. Many dog bites result in an infection and death by a virus called rabies."

"I want to go back home."

"When goats can fly, keep walking. I hear Zohra calling my name."

"Who is she?"

"Zohra is Sadik Batnoon's sister and she is the pillar of the family."

"What do you mean by a pillar of the family? Is she like a building?"

"She is the godmother to the children of the family."

"What is the difference between grandmother and godmother, huh?"

"Grandmother is the mother of a father or mother, while godmother is a woman who promises to take care of a child since birth."

"Do I have a godmother?"

"I am both, your mother and your godmother."

"Gee, it's confusing."

They passed by a café, where a ten-year-old boy, named Bayloe, was sitting outside in the bright sunshine. "Where are you going, and who are you with?"

Joseph shot him a mean look.

"Who is that?" Lima said.

"He is no body much. He wants to embarrass me because I'm with you."

"Is he a friend from school?"

"No! Mother, he is just one of the flunkies at the school. I'm not a dodo to be on the level with such a donkey's head like him."

"What does 'donkey's head' mean?"

"It means double-leg donkey instead of four."

"Don't beat around the bush, boy, answer my question?"

"He is full of crackpot ideas."

"That's pretty much what I imagined!" she said. "Do you know who owns the coffee shop, then?"

"An old man named Pippino owns the cafe."

"Have you been there?"

"No. I haven't. But I saw him loafing around his place."

"Who is that?"

"Pippino—"

"Go on."

"He got a funny nose. His nose would compete with an anteater."

"And what else?"

"He wears a pair of magnifying glasses."

"Well, the man's nose is the star of his face. Four eyes see more than two."

She asked him one more question to check him out if he had ever been in the coffee shop. "Is it a café or coffee shop?"

"I don't know. What is the difference between a café and coffee shop?"

"In a coffee shop, coffee is the main item on the menu. In a café, food like sandwiches is the main item on the menu rather than coffee." She convinced that he had never set foot in the coffee shop.

When they arrived at the Batnoon's abode, around four thirty in the afternoon, Joseph was frozen with fear. His mother knocked on the door, and waited until a woman's voice came from behind the door. "Lima, is that you knocking on the door?"

"Yes, it is."

When the door opened, his eyes closed unconsciously. Something strange happened to Joseph—his eyelids all at once became heavy like lead, as he was unable to control his droopy eyelids. He tried to lift up his pendulous eyelids, but he couldn't. Only shadowy mixtures of light and dark were all that Joseph's eyes could detect; from that moment on he was blind as a bat.

"Welcome Lima and welcome Joseph, we are very pleased to see you both, please come on in," Fatim said. She was wife to Sadik Batnoon.

"Follow me, Joseph," Lima said. Joseph was unable to move or even walk and felt that all of his muscles were immobilized. Suddenly, Lima pulled him inside the doorway as his eyes were purposely shut and his legs were frozen as icicles. When he entered the Batnoon's parlor, he was behaving as a blind mischievous boy. He remained still and silent next to his mother. *"Even the walls have ears, why I can't use my ears instead of my eyes," his mind said.* He began his visit by using his ears instead of his eyes. Joseph used his sense of touch as a glue stick to his mama, only; and pledged to himself not to speak, eat, or drink. While he was sitting next to his mama on the floor cushion, he began to smell smoke inside the parlor, and to hear crackling sound outside the parlor. He detected through his senses of smell and hearing what was happening outside the parlor, and it was nothing but a burning of coal. *"She is igniting charcoal with kerosene in a pottery stove," his awareness said.*

He then heard the clack of heels walking across the parlor. *"The sound of the clack is coming from Zohra's heels, be prepared," his mind said.*

"Hi Joseph, how are you? We are very pleased to have you and your mother as our guests this afternoon," Zohra said.

Zohra's welcoming comment received a mute response by him. He was as mute as a statue in the park.

"How old are you, Joseph?" Zohra said.

"He is seven years old, now," Lima said.

"Is Joseph all right, Lima? His eyes are closed and he doesn't want to talk to me!" Zohra said.

Lima scolded him, and said, "It is cruel to mock a blind person."

He kept silent as a dead-stalled battery.

Lima pinched his arm. "Talk kid talk!"

His mouth appeared as if it was very well connected to his closed eyes.

"He's putting on the face of Pippino without his glasses," Lima said to Zohra.

"Who's Pippino?" Zohra said.

"Joseph told me that he is the owner of the café or the coffee shop, which is on the street to your place," Lima said.

"Is Pippino blind, or what?"

"Joseph told me that he wears thick glasses."

"Then why can't Joseph talk?"

"I guess, cat got his tongue?"

"We must find that cat, then, Lima."

"I am afraid we're not making much progress on that."

"Did he try to pull this stunt before?"

"First time he's acting like a muted bat." She leaned in closer to him and whispered, "You are embarrassing me with your mule-headed stunt. Open your eyes at once."

Joseph sat there as a muted bat, feeling confused, and unsure of himself. Lima and Zohra continued to converse with each other—their long-lasting friendship flowed through them as the conversation filled the air—and he was left to his own devices as a muted bat.

The parlor of the Batnoon's had simple furniture; several tan foam chairs in one corner, and a wooden table with a rotary dial radio on it, in another corner. A massive red carpet was overlaid the marble floor, surrounded by several gray floor cushions, and red silk pillows. The parlor had two large bay windows hidden behind the burgundy velveteen curtains.

There was a fire crackling in the middle of the parlor, spitting out heat and smell of burning charcoal. Joseph strained his ears to catch a strange sound—he heard a sound of slithering underneath the carpet. "Mam, I heard demon sounds, let's take a powder," he whispered.

She lowered her eyebrows and pulled them closer together, and whispered strenuously, "Mama Meow! Open your eyes, then unveil them demons to me!"

"There are goblins with their imps living under the carpet; let's blow out of here."

She pinched his arm as a command to keep quiet.

The alto voices of his mother, Zohra, and Fatim engulfed him, and completely captured his brain. Then he felt fragrant feminine-breaths approaching his face, and a soft gentle hand touching his face. "Hi, Joseph; how are you?"

He didn't reply nor opened his eyes. *He alerted his sixth sense, "Who is she?"*

"Sabria. She is cousin to Mr. Batnoon. She has been blind since birth, not like you," his sixth sense replied.

Lima muttered nervously, "Joseph, answer Sabria. She is talking to you." Then she leaned close to him and whispered in his ear. "Oh, Joseph," she said. "Behave yourself; she is visually impaired. Answer her back."

He whispered back, "What does visually impaired mean?"

"It means blind."

It was a spooky coincidence between his mother and his sixth sense. Both were on the same wavelength channel of their simultaneously broadcasts.

"He doesn't want to see us or talk to us," Fatim told Sabria.

"Leave him be. He is just nervous," Lima said.

He began to hear another type of sound coming from some corner in the parlor—hissing sound. "A snake is hiding in the room, Mother!" he whispered to his mother once again, while he was shaking like a fragile leaf.

She ignored him completely.

"The sound you heard was a sucking sound not a hissing sound. It's a slurping sound made from drinking tea. Everyone is slurping tea like the sound of cats drinking milk in slow motion," his sixth sense explained. He was relieved from his anxiety.

The aroma in the parlor captured Joseph's nose: the tea, and the various pastries. Cake, tea, and refreshments were served at the party. His stomach clenched with hunger at the thought of a piece of delectable cake, nevertheless he kept on closing his mouth, eyes, and his appetite, too. His mother repeatedly encouraged him to open his eyes as the last piece of cake was waiting for him. He ignored all the temptations from his mother, and wished if he could dissolve into the thin air and blow away with the breeze. The parlor was overflowing with sensational and romantic topics, throughout the course of the afternoon party. Their parlor resembled a stage of intriguing melodrama between Fatim, Zohra, Sabria and his mother. He was cast as the only audience member in their parlor, watching them through his ears instead of his eyes.

When it was the time to leave for home; Lima stood up, and said, "Till we meet again, give my best regards to Uncle Sadik."

"Good-bye Lima, and good-bye Joseph, see you both soon," Fatim, and Zohra said consecutively.

Sabria handed him a small plastic bag, smell of sweetness; then kissed him on his sweet cheeks, and said, "This gift is special from me to you, my special one. Good-bye for now, and see you soon."

When Joseph came out of the abode's door, he opened his eyes, and tried to talk to his mother, but she didn't respond to him.

Suddenly they stopped walking when they saw the street was closed off by an ambulance and three police cars. The place was swarmed with police, paramedics, and neighbors. "Oh, no, what's happening there!"

Lima said. They kept walking until a cop stopped them. "You can't go any further, ma'am," a cop said.

"What's happening?" Lima said.

"A dog mauled to death a boy."

"Oh, dang—"

"Yes, ma'am, a boy was killed by a dog."

"Do you know the name of the boy?"

"Sorry, ma'am, I can't reveal the boy's name."

"Much obliged."

"Yes, ma'am—"

Lima and her son took a different route through back streets. When they returned home, Joseph was addled. "That vicious dog killed a boy; I can't believe it!" he said.

"That's the one, next to your grandmother's place," Lima said.

"Are you still upset with me, Mother? Are you going to tell my dad?"

"I'm very upset by your capricious act, this afternoon! I'm not going to mention it to your dad. I'm not an informer."

"I don't know who switched off my sight; I didn't close them on purpose; they closed by themselves. I'm innocent, Mother."

"Fiddle-faddle—"

"I wouldn't fiddle-faddle about that."

"Forget it. Be honest rather than clever." She simmered down.

"Say, that's very swell of you." He was relieved.

That evening, the news spread like wildfire about the boy who was killed by the killer dog . . . that boy was Bayloe. Skye, alias Sepia, the jailbird and the bum owner of the dog was jailed for a serious crime—for unleashing his dangerous dog on the public.

Doorway Five

The Calamity

Prologue

When a tragic memory opens its door, the tears bleed black ink with heartbreak and pain upon the doorway. We write our pain and we understand that writing is not a way to delete it, but a written pain is better than a pent-up pain.

Ode to Rashida

O sunless memory, she was the heart of the family
O sunless memory, she was our three-year-old lighthouse
Her untimely drearily death had driven her family
Into an endless tunnel of cloud covered years
O sunless memory, the suffering of her loss
Defied all the descriptions of bleeding and suffering hearts
O sunless memory, she was an alluring lantern
Illuminated like a star against the black filled-nights
While pouring lightness and warmth to her family
Such an adoring kitten she was
O sunless memory, the dagger of death
You didn't have mercy upon her, did you?
Or let her be
Why death, why? You could have spared her, couldn't you?
O sunless memory, she was just a three-year-old kitten
She was the one who wrapped her heart and soul
Like an anchor, securing her family
O sunless memory, she was an angel

And she was the candlelight of the world
The world of the awakens and the world of memories
Geez, her loving likeness has never faded over the years
Her memory was a tragic reminder
Of a painful reality over the passing years
Geez, Death, alias the Grim Reaper
The invisible-legendary assassin of all time
Appeared to her
As a horrified human skeleton
Masquerading in a shroud and clutching his scythe
Detached her heart
And in cold blood stole her sinless-soul
By his scythe
Then, like a thief in the night
Hijacked her from her family
As a common thief
With his ready jackknife
Stealing our lives as a knife-robbing thief
While your life's reserved-reservoir
Never runs on empty
I loathe the thought of you
But I am fully aware
When I meet up with you
I will reduce you to ruins and to a pile of dust
And gleefully send your ashes back
To your inferno home of everlasting hell
Where you rightfully deserve to burn
Oh sweet oh Rashida
Once after you, the word is dismal
O provider of life
Anyone who eyed your beauty
It is impossible to ever disremember
O blessing of the Creator, O Rashida
Your presence running in our arteries

Oh sweet oh Rashida
O melancholy pounding on in our hearts
If it weren't for your everlasting radiance,
inside our eyes, it wouldn't enlighten
Oh sweet oh Rahida
Until we meet again my dearest Rashida, rest in peace

Grief, solitude, stress, anxiety, and depression are the human ingredients of emotion. These emotions can be subsumed under just one broad category—psychological phenomena. Grief is an emotional pain of losing a loved one and usually associated with/without tears—visible tears could be the audible language of grief; and invisible tears, which drip into the heart, could be the silent tone. Life in general can be a field filled with landmines of emotions between joy and misery—sometimes a sunny day brings happiness, while a cloudy day sometimes brings misery. It is a somber reality that not all humans, especially children, are immune from the pitfalls of grief. Calamity (tragic loss) could lead to the road of solitude—the state of being alone—and it is often associated with mental suffering. Grief could lead to the road of stress (short-term emotional strain) and anxiety (chronic stress). The dead-end freeway of depression (feeling of sadness) merges from two highways: stress and anxiety, respectively.

This is then, the story of Rashida, based, to a large extent, on the flashbacks of her days that Joseph still remembers of them-woven together with strands of blissful times and of grief. He had the gift of time to reflect, time to become an old man, time to open the doorway of her adoring days.

Rashida

The following events took place in mid-spring of 1956, in a city called Addahra. In that city lived a family of five lived in an apartment of a three-story building, where each story had one apartment. They occupied the middle second floor, while the other two Italian families resided in the ground and third floor.

Back in the day when Joseph was six years old, he had a three-year-old sister, named Rashida. She was the enchanting fragrance to her family, and she was protected with overlapping layers of love by her family—namely, Jonah, her father; Lima, her mother; Joseph and Kareem, her two older brothers. She was the adorable child with an angelic face, and magical sparkling brown eyes; her short wavy hair was black as night, shimmering in the sun like the mane of a black filly. Rashida was the affection that built the foundation of her family's love; she was the blooming spring tulip in her family.

The fifty-two-year-old father, Jonah, was six feet two inches tall, well built, with a short-length gray hair. He had one dress code—he wore loose cotton white shirts upon his white trousers with a white cloak, and a flat brimless white cap over his head. The twenty-nine-year-old mother, Lima, was five feet two inches tall, clean limbed, with a black short pixie hairstyle. She had no dress code—she wore different types of brightly colored dresses with no veils. The father was a moderate man, but her mother was a strong-willed woman.

Joseph and his seven-year-old brother, Kareem, looked alike—they were slim built, with short black hair, and brownish eyes. At home they usually wore casual clothes—shorts and T-shirts. Outside of home, they usually dressed in blue jeans, white shirts, and sneakers.

One spring afternoon, while his only sister was playing in the hall of their abode, he heard his mother calling, "Joseph, why don't you come out of your room and play with your little sister?"

"I will, Mother," Joseph said. He whistled happily on his way out of his bedroom, approaching his toddler sister, and said, "Kitty, Kitty, I love you, yes I do."

"Zozo," Rashida babbled. They played together for a while—patty cake, racing a bouncing ball against the wall, hide and seek, and other childhood favorites.

Joseph's bedroom contained a twin bed, studying table with one chair, and a wardrobe for his clothes. Through his bedroom window shined the brightness of the day with the view of the alluring blue sea. When his sister came inside his bedroom, he usually read her a few books, imitating the sound of some animals. "Monkey see, monkey do," he said.

She laughed loudly as Joseph was bobbing up and down like a monkey.

"Mew, meow, mew, meow; baa, baa, baa; moo, moo, moo," he sounded.

She giggled at him as her musical giggles were a sign of her blooming bond toward him.

Joseph sounded quite convincing as a spring chicken, "Cluck cluck, cluck cluck, cluck cluck."

She parroted her brother's different types of sounds and gestures; and that was a sign of her capability to learn.

He slightly held the tip of her ear with his fingers. "Kitty has long ears and a short tongue."

She was immediately alerted, and quickly pulled her ear away from his fingers.

They continued playing together until the voice of his mother came through the door of his bedroom. "Stop playing with your sister, it's time to do your homework."

"Would it be okay if she stayed with me while I do my homework?"

"There are no ifs, ands, or buts for delaying your homework," she said. "Let her be, and pay attention to your homework."

"Okay, mam," he said.

When little Rashida heard her mother's voice, she wobbled out of her brother's bedroom and headed quickly to her mother's side.

As the days passed by, the playtime with his little sister slowly began to diminish. One day, when he came home from school, his mother approached him quietly, and said, "No playtime today with your sister."

"Why is that mam?" Joseph said.

"She is not well, today."

"Can I see her, then?"

"No, you can't see her now, she is taking a nap."

Day by day, the child was hearing the same statement from his mother that his sister was not well.

One day, Joseph asked, "Mother, is Rashida sick?"

"Go to your room and be quiet, don't make any sound, your sister is sleeping," his mother said.

One afternoon, while Joseph was doing his homework, his mother asked him to administer the milk bottle to his sister. He followed his mother into her bedroom where his sister was resting. She was lying on her single bed next to her parents' bed. He quietly approached his sister, and began anxiously to feel worried when he saw her face—her once angelic face was canopied by patches of a blazing red rash.

She opened her eyes, and babbled, "Zozo."

"My sweet Kitty," he said.

His mother showed him how to hold the bottle of milk for her, and then she left the bedroom. What was going on inside of him at that minute was painful, but he was as certain as night follows day that his sister was seriously ill. He held the milk bottle carefully while she was taking in the milk from the baby bottle. A few minutes later she tiredly turned her silent mouth away from the nipple of the half full bottle, adoringly looked up at him, and then closed her trusting eyes.

Thereafter, the afternoon routine, when Joseph returned from school was to help his mother with the milk bottle, and that was a precious time to be with his little sister. The first question that came into Joseph's mind when he returned from school, each day, was to inquire about his sister's condition. It was painfully clear to him that his mother was playing hide-and-seek with her answers.

One day Lima muttered sadly, "Your little sister is sick." Her eyes crinkled. "Oh, Joseph," she said. "Your sister is sick."

"What's wrong with her?" said Joseph.

"I don't know now, I don't know, I don't know . . . just take the milk to her; I am so busy right now in the kitchen."

"Okay, Mother." He grabbed the warm baby bottle by both hands, and scampered like a cat, lightly and quietly, to his sister's bedside.

Joseph was alarmed when he saw his sister that afternoon. Her face, arms, and her legs were blanketed with the red-rash. "Hi, little one," he said.

Rashida's eyes glimmered with watery tears, and that was her only response.

He wiped her tears with a tissue, "Dear Rashida." He gave her the bottle. "Here you go," he said. "You'll be just fine." Then he kneeled on the carpet, leaned toward her, and carefully rolled his cheek beside her face. After she drifted off to sleep, he took the milk bottle, which was still half full, and then fell fast asleep. They slept as two bonded kittens while their mother was alone in the kitchen preparing the evening-meal for the family.

"After I put the broth on the stove, I'll check on the kids." Lima whispered to herself.

A few minutes later, Lima heard her daughter crying. *"Now, it's time for an inspection," she said.* She left the kitchen, dashed to her daughter's room, and opened the bedroom door. She saw her daughter was crying excessively, while her son, Joseph, was slumbering like a hibernated bear. His silent head was tilted on the edge of the bed and the nipple of the milk bottle was securely in his mouth to boot. Apparently, he fed himself quite nicely, instead of his little sister.

She quickly picked-up her daughter from the bed, hugged and comforted her; then looked at her son with annoyance while he was in dreamland. "Aha, wake up bad boy!" she said. "Is that all you have done, a nap after a snack! I thought you were going to help me! You are as helpless as a fish out of water."

He woke up soaked with confusion. "Uh, Mother, I'm . . . Mother."

"No ellipses, what happened?"

"What do you mean by that, Mother?"

"No missing words, just a straight answer; what happened since you came here to feed your sister?"

"I don't know, Mother, what really happened."

"I know what happened; I know you drank the whole bottle. That's what I know."

"Uh . . . I don't know, maybe the baby bottle liked me more than Kitty."

"You don't know what you are talking about. You will never be trusted with the milk bottle again. Go on, with you. Get."

"All right, swell." Then, swiftly, he darted outside to the hallway and went to his bedroom. He was off the hook this time.

There was a limited and primitive government operated outpatient clinic, walking distance from the family's apartment. The outpatient clinic was located on the ground floor of a big compound and was relying on the council of the town to operate it. The nineteen century stylish clinic had only one large room, where the general practitioner was seeing his patients; and one large hall for the nurse, where he/she was treating the patients. The clinic's operational hours were Saturday–Thursday, 8:00 a.m.–3:00 p.m. There was no need for an appointment to see a GP or a nurse as the policy of the clinic was primarily based on first come, first serve. The clinic was known by an alias The Tree Doctor; no one knows from where that strange alias came from; but it most likely got its alias from that big oak tree that was in the clinic garden. The clinic was the focus of the neighborhood; and it was crowded in the mornings and less crowded after mid-day. The clinic provided health care for all, based on their need for medical care rather than their ability to pay. The clinic was offering routine check-ups and limited treatments for non-serious cases; whereas serious cases were referred to a specialist in the main hospital.

One afternoon around two o'clock while he was doing his homework, his mother rushed into his bedroom, and said, "I need to take your sister to The Tree Doctor; and I want you to keep an eye on Kahloosha."

"What's with my sister?" Joseph said.

"She is too feverish."

"Go ahead, take her to the clinic, I am real willing to keep an eye on the maid."

His mother wrapped her arms around her sick baby daughter, then left the apartment in a panic state, and went directly to the neighborhood clinic—The Tree Doctor.

The maid, Kahloosha, was a young black woman, mid-twenties, tall, slim, with medium and curly black-hair. Her voice echoed like a deep drum, powerful enough to make everyone's bones feel like they were vibrating. It was as if the scent of African incense had soaked her heated body and was lingering in the air for her fingerprint identification. She was employed by Lima to do some domestic work, six days a week, except for Fridays. She had one dress code, a white apron on a black long dress. Her performance tasks were cooking, vacuuming, cleaning the floors and surfaces, un-dusting the household, and washing and ironing the family's clothes. The maid dreaded each Thursday, because it was the day to do laundry. Early days, the laundry method was widely practiced by washing clothes by hand in a large wash tub, hanging them on a clothesline, and then pressing them. It was a tedious task, especially for a large family. The maid was playing the mouse-and-cat game with Lima—she used to pretend to be very diligent about her work in front of her employer, but she would take another turn when Lima was out of her sight.

After his mother and his baby sister left the apartment, Joseph returned back to his daily homework and locked the door of his room. For no apparent reason, he never liked nor disliked Kahloosha; she was nobody much to him. He snubbed her completely without fear or without reproach from his mother.

After he completed his daily math homework, he came out of his bedroom to discover that the maid was sleeping in the hall like a bag of charcoal lying on a floor cushion, making her head at home. He stuttered for a moment with his eyes opened, every part of him went on pause. The sense of laziness of the slumbering maid triggered his mind to do something unusual that he never did before or since his childhood, except when he played football. Unaware of what he was about to do, he started to kick the maid in her legs while she was dreaming away in her afternoon nap. The alarmed kicks from his foot were the alarm clock for the maid's drowsy head. She woke up confused as in a dream gone wrong, looked at him with her bug eyes, and then frowned. He saw rage-stirred waves in her bulging eyes, and momentarily his sixth sense told him to stay put. "You should be working not napping," he mumbled.

She frowned, looked up at him square in the eye, and said furiously, "That's a devil of a way."

"For being lazy—"

"You little squirt."

"Little squirt, huh?"

"Yeah, little squirt."

He felt like he was underwater. "Now, get."

She hopped up on the floor cushion like a kangaroo, wrapped her scarf around her head, and said, "I hate ya, little squirt."

"Like wise. Get."

"This is it. I got to get."

"Go on, then."

"Pshaw." She left the apartment as if a lightening had struck her, and fled down the flight of stairs like a thief into the night.

When Lima came back home with her baby daughter from The Tree Doctor; she found her son was anxiously waiting in the hallway for the news about his sick sister.

"How's Kitty, Mother?" he said.

"Well, your sister is not seriously ill," she said.

"Swell."

"Uh-huh."

"What The Tree Doctor said?"

She said sadly, "He said 'It's very common for toddlers to get rashes.'" Her eyes bleared. "He gave her a prescription," she said. "And before we left, the nurse gave her an injection . . . a nurse will come by every day to give her an injection." Then she headed with her sleepy daughter to her bedroom and shut the door.

She came out of her bedroom, calling the maid's name, and then went to Joseph's bedroom. "Where is Kahloosha?"

He was baffled, and said, "Well, Mother—"

"Well, what?"

"Well, Mother—"

"Stop mothering around me. Where is she?

"She left."

"Left where?"

"I don't know."

"She is doing the laundry on the roof, isn't she?"

"She is not upstairs."

"Where is she, then?"

"I told you, Mother . . . she left the apartment."

"When did she leave?"

He decided to go out on a limb. "I found her sleeping in the hall; and when I woke her up she called me 'little squirt.'"

His mother stared open-mouthed at him.

"Believe you me; she called me 'little squirt,' flat out."

"That's a foul-mouthed way of speaking."

"Yes, Mother."

"What happened, then?"

"I gave her the boot."

"Watch your language, boy."

"I asked her to leave, Mother."

"And she left."

"Uh-huh."

"Well, I don't like your story; tell me another one."

"There is no other story, except the one that I have told you, Mother."

"Well, I don't want to jump the gun and throw the book at you before I see Kahloosha this coming Saturday."

"Yes." He acted calm on the surface, because he wanted his mother to buy his cock and bull story about how the maid left the apartment.

"Have you done all your homework yet?"

"Yes, Mother."

She nodded her head up and down at him, and said, "Always remember, true success is one percent intelligence and ninety-nine percent hard work. Who toils, succeeds; and who plants, reaps." Then she left him alone with his thoughts in his bedroom.

Days had passed and Joseph was on pins and needles that the maid would show up and spill the beans on him to his mother. Luckily, his cock and bull story was never detected by his mother, as no one from the family ever laid eyes on Kahloosha again, like she was swallowed up by quicksand and vanished without trace.

Nurse Rosa visited Rashida every day and provided her with a penicillin injection and applied some type of a cream for her skin rash. Rosa was a short and slender Italian nurse. She was dressed in regular clothes—a gray skirt below the knee, short-sleeved white blouse, and black ankle length stockings with white nursing shoes. Her salt-and-pepper short hair was covered with a white headscarf pulled tight beneath her chin. The glasses on her snub nose gave her that wide-eyed silent and focused appearance, even though she was a petite middle-aged woman. She had a rectangular black leather case, which apparently contained medications. The treatment continued for seven days, after which Rashida's condition partially improved; but after ten days of receiving the medical treatment, a mysterious illness began to whisper into her fragile body. She became bedridden, suffering from a high-grade fever, pain, and severe skin rash. A plague of panic among the family became palpable in their physical and emotional senses.

The family waited cautiously for a few days until one day she became more seriously ill. That day, her father wrapped his frail daughter up in his arms, and went straight to the town's main hospital's emergency room. "We are just going to draw blood from her to check for few things," the ER doctor said.

"Tell me, Doctor, what type of a disease does she have?" Jonah said.

"The blood test will tell if she has an infection or not."

Five tubes of blood samples were collected by phlebotomy from her tiny vein. The phlebotomist gave her a shot in her buttock, and subsequently she became better. After that, Jonah wrapped her up in his arms and headed for home.

Lima, Joseph, and Kareem stood in the apartment doorway, waiting for Jonah and Rashida to return. "How is our beautiful baby girl?" Lima said.

"She is fine; she will be fine. They took a blood-sample; the results will come after that," said Jonah.

Few days later, the blood results revealed that Rashida had developed German measles (rubella) and her white blood cells (leukocytes) were very low. Her blood test results had come as a heart-breaking shock to her beloved family.

When Jonah went to the hospital to get the blood test results, the doctor told him, "Your daughter was infected by a virus called rubella/German measles. This virus is spread through air—"

"Is there a cure for this virus?" said Jonah.

"Well, there is no specific treatment for it. It has to run its course; however, I will prescribe penicillin for her."

"She has already had penicillin."

"When was that?"

"It was ten days ago."

"She needs another dosage of penicillin for the next seven days," the doctor said. "The red blood cells, the plasma, and the platelets are normal; but the white blood cells, which protect the body from infection, are mighty low."

"How does a person get this disease?"

"German measles/rubella is caused by a virus in the air."

"Is that so?"

"Yes, a virus lingering in the air; not by bacteria, though."

"What is the difference between German measles and rubella?"

"The disease known as the German measles, because it was first recorded in Germany; measles meaning 'many little spots' and the name 'rubella' was originated from the Latin word that means 'little red', two different names for one disease."

"She got it from the air, huh?"

"It is a contagious disease and can be passed by an infected person through talking, sneezing and coughing. You are more than welcome, Jonah, to come and see me if your daughter' symptoms persist. I will also prescribe her something for her fever, cough syrup. Keep an eye on her temperature and give her plenty of fluids, plenty of water."

"Much appreciated, Doctor, for your professional assistance, Doctor; I am mighty obliged to you. Good-bye," Jonah said. Then, he left the hospital.

Nurse Rosa showed up for the second time and began to administer the penicillin to Rashida. In the first few days of treatment, Rashida's health improved slightly—her high temperature dropped to normal, but the red spots on her body did not disappear. A week later following the treatment, a new state of tension and a cloud of doom hovered over the horizon of the household as there was little hope of improvement in her health. She became totally bedridden with fever, causing the family to be on the cliff of despair. Later, she began to cry out as she was pleading for mercy. At night her temperature would rise to 102 degrees Fahrenheit (approximately, thirty-nine degrees Celsius). The booster penicillin injections and the syrup couldn't lower her temperature, and her skin rash had remained unchanged. All the three combined treatments were failing her.

Stealthily, Joseph began to approach his stricken sister every day, standing by her bedside, and looking down at her in hellish agony. One particular day, he was in a state of shock, when he saw his sister without a nightgown and her fragile body was inflamed in red. He heard her moaning and saw how she was shivering like the last leaf of autumn. The image of what he witnessed sent a shiver down to his spine, vibrating through every inch in his muscular movement, and derailed his train of reality.

One intense night, Rashida was shivering with cold and unable to swallow any blended food including water. A physician was called from the local hospital; he examined her carefully, and said, "She has scarlet fever."

"I'll be doggoned. The hospital told us that she had German measles," said Jonah.

"She has swollen tonsils and red bumpy tongue and sever shivering; these symptoms indicate a scarlet fever rather than German measles," he said. "Keep a warm towel around her neck to relief the swollen tonsils." He gave her drops of antibiotic in her mouth.

"Sure, we will do that."

"I'm going to give her a prescription for more antibiotics. The drug should be taken orally every six hours for a week."

"We thank you most kindly."

"It's my obligation; hope she gets better." Then, he left.

Jonah looked at his wife, and said, "To know the disease is half the cure." At once, the parents were thrown into a panic state of confusion between the German measles and the Scarlet fever.

Late one night, Joseph was surprised when he noticed his Aunt Eve, Jonah's younger sister, was sitting on the pinky-shaded wing-back chair in the living room as he came out from his bedroom. She was on the chunky side, pale skin tone, and had an oily complexion with black bulging bug-eyes; she wore a long plain gray dress with a white non-flattering scarf on her melon-shaped head. He noticed that neither his parents nor Rashida were at home.

"Where is everyone, Aunt Eve?" said Joseph.

"They went to the hospital," Eve said. "An ambulance was here earlier and took them to the hospital while you were sleeping in your bedroom." Her answer skyrocketed over his head like a sonic boom.

He knew that his sister was a prisoner trapped in her own suffering torment, which made him feel weary with despair.

She tried cleverly to change the subject, as some people change one subject to conceal another. "Show me your secret stash of toys, Joseph."

"Hmm . . . who told you that I have a secret stash?"

"You have a gun, haven't you?"

"Yes, I have a cap gun."

"Show it to me, then."

"All right, swell, you asked for it." He didn't feel the need to boast about his cap gun, but he had no choice other than to show it to her. He ambled back to his bedroom, fetching the cap gun from his bedroom, and returned back to his stodgy aunt.

He aimed his cap gun directly at his aunt's right temple, and discovered that she was dozing. She was snoring like a pair of squeaky old boots while her head tilted on the winged side of the pinky wingback chair. He tip-toed quietly back to his bedroom.

Around midnight, Joseph heard his parents in the hall. He rushed out from his room to greet them. "Where is Rashida?"

"She is in good hands. She is in the hospital," Lima said.

He asked his mother if he could visit his sister and deliver her favorite doll, so she wouldn't feel quite so lonely.

"There is no visitation for children under the age of twelve; your father and I are the only ones allowed to visit your sister," she said.

He pleaded with his parents to be allowed to see his baby sister.

"It's the hospital regulations. You can't come with us," Jonah said.

"Where is Aunt Eve?" Joseph said.

"She left; and now go back to bed," Lima said.

He wandered off back to his room while the fear of the unknown was invading every cell in his heart.

After ten days, Rashida came back home from the hospital. Day after day her parents and her brothers waited in vain for her to get well; but she didn't. She had a relentless fever all of the time, even though she took different array of medications. Jonah had an unshakable premonition that the silhouette of death was hovering over his only daughter.

One evening Rashida was crying excessively, throbbing with lingering pain. A doctor was called at once. He gave her another injection, and said, “She will be fine.”

“Fine, fine, fine . . . fine what? Her frail body is a road map full of needle marks; these useless injections haven’t done any good for her; instead her health is deteriorating after each injection,” Lima said.

“Doctor, I would sell everything I own in this life; I just want my little baby girl to get well!” Jonah said.

The doctor was enticed by Jonah’ statement, and said, “You are a refined gentleman, Jonah, don’t give up hope.” Then, he left the apartment.

One gloomy evening, Joseph saw his mother in the hall crying hysterically and beating with her shaky hands on her cheeks like a war drum. He muttered nervously, “Why are you crying, Mother?” His voice strangled with fear. “Oh, Mother,” he said. “Please stop crying and scratching your cheeks, you are really frightening me!”

She couldn’t utter a single syllable as she was falling in a mourning state of mind; and shut down from her barely existing surroundings. Obviously, she was in a catatonic spiraling tunnel that impeded her speaking—she was muted. She barely could walk back into her bedroom. That unforgettable evening, the family was bulldozed by a distraught catastrophe.

Next morning, Joseph witnessed a physician leaving his sick baby sister’s room, while his mother was pleading in a hysterical tone of voice and in an imploring potent demand. “I beg you, Jonah, tell the doctor to wake her up, she needs me, I don’t know what has happened to her! No one, no one, and I mean no one can steal my baby girl from me, hear.”

“Okay, okay, Lima,” Jonah said.

Pouting sadly, the doctor padded Jonah on his shoulder, and then walked off.

Jonah looked heartbroken to Joseph and Kareem. “You are not

going to school today . . . I need you both to stay at home . . . your mother needs us."

Dramatically, Lima dropped on the marble floor, screaming and kicking like a woman who lost her mind. "O God, protect my baby."

Jonah grabbed and lifted her from the floor, taking her into their bedroom, and locked the door.

Joseph and Kareem were not prepared for this shocking and horrifying revelation. Their knees were shaking like a rattle and their legs were galvanized to their baby sister's door.

Late Friday evening, during that early spring, Rashida let out her final sigh of relief—she left the mortal life and her angelic soul departed to the heavens of the eternal life.

The entire family was left disorientated by her premature death. They plunged into a deep dark tunnel of inescapable depression. That was the new norm—everything was in a topsy-turvy atmosphere—they had to live with it, and they may have to die with it.

By then, Lima was crying without warning, completely overcome with grief. Then, a note of hysteria crept into her voice—she began to scream, thrashing her cheeks and face by her own finger nails. Jonah's main response was to stay strong for the family.

Next day, around one o'clock, Rashida's body was moved to the bathroom for the final bathing. The bathing was given by Nurse Rosa—she washed Rashida's body, shampooed her hair, and then towel dried her. Next, she carried Rashida's body back to her death-bed. Jonah trailed Rosa into the bedroom, while her mother was lying unconscious in her bed. The nurse applied Rashida's body with a springtime-scented perfume, combing her thick-soft-black hair, and then placed a white satin bow headband around her head. Finally, she dressed Rashida with one of her lovely heavenly satin white dress.

"Nurse, would you please give my wife something before she wakes up?" Jonah said.

The nurse was very cooperative and gave the unconscious Lima another injection that would put her into a soundless state of sleep for a few merciful hours.

Around three o'clock on that black Friday, Rashida was carried out of her bedroom by her father, while her mother remained unaware of what was happening. There was no coffin for Rashida—her body was wrapped in a white blanket in her father's loving and protective arms as he joyfully carried her when she was full of life. Her brothers, Joseph and Kareem, were sobbing out of control with outstretched arms to prevent their father from taking away their precious younger sister. Both brothers were in a state of shock and disbelief as they witnessed their lifeless sweet sister leaving the family-home for the last time.

A wise man can always be found alone; and their father fit the format without hesitation. The cemetery was within walking distance from their home. Jonah walked self-possessed for about twenty minutes while he was cradling his lifeless baby daughter between his arms. A handful of onlookers attended her solemn procession as her illness and sudden death were kept a secret from the neighborhood. The procession was on foot and led by her father until it moved into the cemetery.

At the cemetery, a rectangular hole was waiting for her. Jonah refused to release her, holding her tight between his trembling arms, and couldn't let her go from his cradling arms. After fifteen minutes, he reluctantly agreed to hand over his daughter to a mourner. The mourner lowered her body slowly into her grave, laying her two favorite dolls beside her body. Jonah looked tearfully upon her, while she was lying in her grave, and said grievously, "I took you my sweet baby from your temporary mother to your lasting mother . . . the earth is our lasting mother . . . that's a fact of life and we must accept it. Your eternal mother has just beckoned you back-home and soon we will follow you . . . my sweet baby . . . rest in peace . . . my only Rashida. There is no mighty and there is no power but from God."

Rashida was born in the spring, and died in the spring as a spring daffodil. The three springs of Rashida's life would never be buried away by time. The grief swept through her family as a river in mountain passes, eroding their happiness, and created a new chapter of a sorrowful-life. Her mother eroded the most from life—she rocked back and forth in her grief, mumbling in delirium day and night. She had fallen to the floor several times. She was out-of-character mentally and physically. Nurse Rosa visited her daily, giving her antidepressant medications and injections for her erratic behavior and constant wailing.

Lima's sobbing, next to her daughter's empty bed, was much the same twenty-four hours/seven days. Her health deteriorated and she was unable to cope with reality and daily life routines. One day Nurse Rosa addressed her concerns for Lima. "Jonah, your wife doesn't need me any longer; she needs the immediate care of a psychiatrist."

Jonah thanked her, but felt ashamed and embarrassed about the word psychiatrist. Later that day, he came with an idea of providing his wife with liquor and tobacco instead of letting her to see a psychiatrist—mental illness during that era was a taboo subject.

Epilogue

Lima started drinking alcohol and smoking cigarettes most of the time at night in complete secrecy—no one knew about it except her husband, Jonah. With abnormal usage of alcohol and tobacco, her condition didn't improve, but rather worsened. Lima's lingering sadness grew deeper and deeper inside her until she became an embedded root for a weeping willow tree of sadness. She cried like a travailing woman, wearing black mourning dresses for countless years to come, and became emotionally and physically detached from reality and her own surroundings. In those days wearing black mourning dresses was a sign of detachment from social events and a signal to be left alone. She was lost in the woods of grief—she became very scared of others, of the world, of being vulnerable all the time. She lost weight, her skin turned pale, her eyes puffed up from the intensity of crying, and her once well-styled black hair had been replaced by unkempt straggling gray hair. She detested both feasts and holidays. She lost her appetite for food and her will-to-live. Grievance veiled her as a fog from the reality that her daughter had departed this life. The nights were by far her meditative-time of each day—sitting on her window-seat, by her opened bedroom window, watching and conversing to the moon, until the wee small hours of each morning. She lived behind the mirror, not in front of the mirror.

Coping with a sick wife and two youngsters was very draining on Jonah. Although he was marginally better than his wife, he hid his grievance inside his heart.

Joseph and Kareem had received an exorbitant dosage of tragedy at an early stage of their developing years. They were like two confused butterflies that were tangled in a net of grief. Their once carefree childhood memories were lost forever from their innocent impressionable minds.

Rashida's calamitous death was an everlasting reminder of the unwanted gift of grief upon her family. Her mother lost her spice for life, her father felt like he had a bullet embedded inside his heart, and her two brothers felt besotted by her tragic death. Calamitously, she died at age of three . . . and that was the eternal calamity, which shadowed the entire family.

www.ingramcontent.com/pod-product-compliance
Lightning Source LLC
LaVergne TN
LVHW010621100826
845148LV00014B/3059
* 9 7 8 1 7 3 7 4 9 4 1 0 2 *